THE JEM'HADAR PHASERS STRUCK THE DEFIANT . . .

. . . And Commander Benjamin Sisko's ship rocked under the steady fire.

"Direct hit off the port nacelle," a crewman shouted.

"Disengage cloak!" Sisko ordered. "Raise shields, prepare to fire on my command!"

Again the powerful alien weapons struck, and smoke filled the bridge.

"Report!" Sisko shouted.

Clipped professional voices answered him. "Sensors are out!" "Starboard power coupling destroyed!" "Rerouting main power!"

Grimly, Sisko considered the situation. "Lock on to the lead ship," he ordered, knowing the chances of surviving were slim to none. "Fire at will!"

Look for STAR TREK Fiction from Pocket Books

Star Trek: The Original Series

Star Trek: The Next Generation

Star Trek: Deep Space Nine

STAR TREK
DEEP SPACE NINE®

THE SEARCH

A Novel by Diane Carey
Based on THE SEARCH: Part I
Story by Ira Steven Behr & Robert Hewitt Wolfe
Teleplay by Ronald D. Moore
AND
THE SEARCH: Part II
Story by Ira Steven Behr & Robert Hewitt Wolfe
Teleplay by Ira Steven Behr

POCKET BOOKS

New York   London   Toronto   Sydney   Tokyo   Singapore

An *Original* Publication of POCKET BOOKS

POCKET BOOKS, a division of Simon & Schuster Inc.
1230 Avenue of the Americas, New York, NY 10020

STAR TREK is a Registered Trademark of Paramount Pictures.

This book is published by Pocket Books, a division of Simon & Schuster Inc., under exclusive license from Paramount Pictures.

ISBN: 0-671-50604-8

First Pocket Books printing October 1994

10 9 8 7 6 5 4 3 2 1

POCKET and colophon are registered trademarks of Simon & Schuster Inc.

Printed in the U.S.A.

THE SEARCH

CHAPTER
1

"DIRECT HIT on the docking ring!"

Jem'Hadar. The new scourge. Here they came again.

A venomous ship swung in on an almost head-on course, weapons hacking at open space even before they homed in on the command tower of the space station, and they loved what they were doing.

"They're punching right through the new shields!" Major Kira Nerys felt her throat burn with raw frustration. She was less announcing than grinding out a damnation.

Clinging to his console at Engineering as another hit made the whole deck throb, Miles O'Brien bent forward to keep his balance. "There's a hull breach in sections twenty-three alpha through sixteen baker. Heavy casualties."

"Try boosting power to the interface. Maybe if we can—"

The Ops bulkhead exploded. Shrapnel whistled across the area, slicing a half dozen crewmen down like a twister through corn. Warning of hull breach howled in their ears.

"Transporters are out," O'Brien coughed. Forcing himself to spare two sore fingers, he tapped the nearest comm. "Medical team to Ops."

Kira saw him in the corner of her eye, and almost went for her own comm unit to call for medical help, then suddenly realized he had just done that.

Under usual conditions she would've been the one to do that. But there wasn't anybody here to give her orders. She was in charge of the disintegration of Station *Deep Space Nine*.

At moments like this she wished she had some nice long hair to tear out. She would've gladly left auburn knots all over the deck.

Just for a couple of seconds she wanted hair. Lots of it.

The station rocked again. Plasma residue cascaded past the observation portals, creating fireworks almost celebratory. Their lights flashed on the bodies of the fallen Ops crewmen.

"Where the hell are the runabouts?" Kira choked. "The *Mekong*'s supposed to be defending grid two-one-five!"

"*Mekong*'s lost her port nacelle, sir," O'Brien said, his voice painfully calm. "The *Rio Grande*'s been destroyed . . . and the *Orinoco* is still engaged with a Jem'Hadar ship near the wormhole—"

He was thrown to one side by another hit.

Incredible—these bolts that could shake the entire station—virtually punching a city with one fist. The lights wobbled. In the unsteady flickers of struggling conduits Kira could barely see O'Brien's face.

In the background the turbolift burped halfway open, then all the way. Julian Bashir and his medical team stumbled onto the command deck, were startled for a moment at the unrecognizable area that moments ago had been the neat, clean brain of DS9, then gathered their nerves and separated to triage the wounded.

Kira blinked, flashing back to the moment she had watched Julian die on the holosuite. That had only happened in one simulation and it still plagued her to watch the doctor fall. He was the most innocent of heart among them, one of those of kind nature, and watching him die had made her mad.

But all her friends and countrymen would die if *Deep Space Nine* failed to defend the only bridge to the Gamma Quadrant. If they only possessed the firepower, the wormhole was tactically ideal, but it was like waiting for the monster to come in the window.

"All right," Kira called across to O'Brien, "concentrate our fire on the lead ship in each wave. Use defense pattern echo-one-five with torpedoes set to—"

The whole station shifted a full ten feet to her right, and she almost went down. Her hips cranked so hard beneath her that she bruised her own ribs, and that was the only way she stayed on her feet. Around her, almost everyone else went down. Some skidded along the deck and struck torn pieces of dislodged bulkhead and console facings.

The lights flickered again, and this time went out. Darkness swelled like a wound.

"Main power's off-line," O'Brien shouted, his voice weaker than the last time. "Shields are gone, no power to the weapons—"

Kira was about to shout back that she didn't want any more reports. She had to think about what she did have instead of what she didn't. Of course, that was the basic idea behind those kinds of damage reports—to know what to use—but right now she didn't care. Reflex kicked in and she started thinking like an underground fighter again.

What could she use? Could she gather hand phasers and tap their energy stores? Were there welding torches on the station? Knives? Chemicals?

She parted her lips to tell him what to do, though she had no idea what was going to come out of there. She trusted to her instincts to pop up with something.

But she would never know whether or not she was up to that moment's demands.

Three bands of transporter energy seared into shape on the Operations deck. An instant later, three gray-masked aliens with weapons drawn opened fire on station personnel.

Kira sucked a hard gasp as Julian Bashir and one of his medical aides were ground to death under

Jem'Hadar energy beams. Another second, and the rest of the medical team was dead too.

Across the deck, O'Brien shook his head and sighed.

Kira rushed out from behind her station and leveled a kick and a half dozen punches at the nearest Jem'Hadar soldier, who took each blow stoically. He barely felt her assault.

Another soldier leveled his weapon at O'Brien and fired. The beam passed through his body.

Still kicking, Kira gritted her teeth then stumbled back a pace or two.

The computer voice had a slight echo. *"Unable to continue simulation. There is no data available on Jem'Hadar physical strength or endurance."*

The voice was so damned polite it might as well have said, "Thank you for not spitting on the deck."

"Oh, shut up," Kira sniffed. "End simulation."

The entire Ops center winked out, leaving a velvet black holosuite. On the deck, Julian's body and the forms of the other med staffers faded away.

Eyes lingering on the places where they had lain slaughtered, Kira shifted back and forth. The damning reality of this thing plagued her. She could train and train, but would she be able to act when the real thing came along? She could experience the horrors of war firsthand, but was that good? Would she freeze when the real thing came along? Bravery was often born of spontaneous inexperience. She could be destroying that for herself.

She certainly wasn't getting anything out of this.

O'Brien sighed again and didn't say anything.

"Chief," Kira muttered, "I'm getting tired of losing."

He wandered toward her. "Sorry, Major. I really thought we had it this time."

"Sorry's not good enough," she snapped. "The Dominion could have an entire invasion fleet sitting on the other side of the wormhole for all we know. We need a way to fight off a Jem'Hadar assault and we need it now."

Fatigue blistered O'Brien's otherwise affable expression, but he nodded as though he knew she was right. "Yes, sir. I'll begin working on some alternatives."

He didn't say the rest of what was lingering on that sentence—that there weren't very many alternatives left, short of poison or witchcraft.

For the thousandth time—today—she remembered her time in the underground and how since then she had thought those bad days were finally over. Now these new changes . . . did she have the fight left in her anymore?

If the Dominion showed up and Starfleet backed off . . . what if Starfleet didn't concentrate a fleet here? What if they came up with excuses to avoid defending her home planet, way out here by itself in the middle of deep space, without much in the way of value?

What did the Federation value? Wheat? Iron? Latinum?

She wasn't sure. And it was possible she didn't want to know.

Starfleet could move, but Bajor couldn't. Her

home planet and its desperately poor people, clawing their way back up from oppression, just didn't have much left to fight with. If push came to shove, Bajor would be back on its own again, and she would be a rat in the dirt again with pretty slim chances of survival if the Dominion took over this sector.

Because she knew . . . she would never give in to them.

And she knew other things, truths lurking in the back of her attempts to defend the station. Occupation forces, concentration camps, mass murder, the spare life of the underground, day-by-day sacrifice. There were factions in the Federation who measured the galaxy by whole star systems and whole sectors, not by one or two planets dotting a frontier.

In her tactician's heart of hearts, Kira knew where the planet Bajor stood on the roster of the critical. Starfleet would be foolish to sacrifice a whole fleet to defend a planet that just wasn't important enough.

If she were at Starfleet Command, given trust to scope out a defense plan for a quarter of a galaxy, what would she decide?

Contempt for the distant hub was tempered as she thought of how hesitant Bajor had been to join the Federation, how resentful of encroachment, how some Bajorans had treated Starfleet's liberation forces with as much acrimony as they had treated the Cardassians' occupation. The desire to be completely independent had burrowed in too far, and even when they needed help to stabilize and rebuild, they had remained inhospitable and isolationist. They wanted to be Bajoran with a capital B, to strut for a while, to prove to themselves that they could stand alone and spit upon the hand held out to them by the Federation.

Just for a while, just a tease.

Now this.

She had to find a way to defend Bajor from the station, or the station from Bajor. All she had to do was tip the odds in favor of her own planet and this station, and Starfleet might find it worthwhile to defend Bajor.

She led the way down the narrow stairs to Quark's bar, noting with a resentful shiver that the stairs were barely wide enough for two humanoids to walk down together and that the width was calculated to make those two humanoids bump each other tenderly with every step. Bothered by what the holosuites up there were most often used for—not exactly battle simulation—she leaned away from O'Brien, anticipating that a settled family man might be embarrassed to bump once too often.

For her the whole technology of simulation was a double-edged sword. Simulations so real that soldiers could train for battle, yes; but so often true heroism was a product of naïveté, of not realizing how much battle really hurt, and how much it really hurt to watch friends die.

The holodeck might make a training soldier too cautious. What eighteen-year-old would go to war if he had already experienced what war could be? So much heroism came from hard, fast lessons in danger's jaws. . . .

"On the plus side," she said as they finally made it down the long stairway to the crowded, murmuring bar, "your new runabout deployment plan seemed to at least slow them down before they could get to the station."

She stopped, seeing the snaggletoothed Ferengi proprietor angling to intercept them, carrying a bill.

"Yes, sir," O'Brien said. "I think if we open up the interval between the runabouts to five hundred meters, it might buy us another thirty seconds."

"Are you two finished up there?" Quark interrupted. "I've been turning away customers—customers who paid in *advance,* I might add—for three hours."

"Good idea," Kira said to O'Brien, ignoring the twisted look Quark gave her when he thought she was talking to him. Quark liked to think that all women of all species were always talking to him.

"Speaking of paying," the Ferengi went on, "who's going to pick up this bill for three days of holosuite activity?"

O'Brien talked over Quark's head. Well, over his ears. "There might also be a way to boost our deflector field integrity if we run it through an antimatter processor."

"And I hope," Quark went on, "you're not going to tell me to charge it to the Bajoran government."

"Try it," Kira clipped. Annoyed, she tried to look past him to O'Brien and concentrate on the analysis of defense. They were all about to die and here was Quark yammering about getting paid as if he didn't comprehend. This wasn't casual conversation, and she wanted Quark out of it, even for his own sake. The Ferengi would be shaken if he knew what they had been planning, and what they anticipated.

"Because getting money out of them is like trying to get blood from a Tholian," Quark was saying.

They'd managed to wander toward the door. "Now, when Commander Sisko returns from Starfleet Headquarters," Kira went on to O'Brien, "I want you to give him a full briefing on all the technical modifications that you and I—"

"Major!" Nervous that they might get out into the corridor without paying, Quark suddenly planted himself squarely in their path. "I'm afraid I have to insist on an answer. Now, what am I supposed to do with this bill?"

He held it up in front of her.

Kira's elbow tingled with desire as she imagined it about four inches down his throat. No, that wouldn't do. She was in charge of the station. Image to maintain and all that.

Blast it.

She managed a completely fake, completely sweet smile. "I'll tell you what you can do with that bill, Quark," she said. The smile melted. "Or would you like me to demonstrate it?"

Quark's expression wobbled and he dropped back a step.

It wasn't that unique a trick, but something about her was convincing. Kira leaned toward him to clarify her point, but the chirp of her comm badge interrupted her.

The sophisticated voice of Jadzia Dax called, "Dax to Major Kira."

Kira touched the badge. "Kira."

"Have you forgotten something, Major?"

She glanced at O'Brien. "Forgotten what?"

"You called a tactical briefing for sixteen hundred. It's sixteen-twenty. We're all here waiting."

"Oh—yes, I forgot! We'll be right there—sorry."

"Noted. Dax out."

"I don't believe it!" Her mind preoccupied with the idea of invasion, Kira bumped O'Brien again as the two of them dodged for the exit, but this wasn't the kind of bump that made her self-conscious.

As they ran full-out down the throbbing deck, she heard Quark call after them.

"I'll put it on your tab!"

"We're in trouble, people."

Grim and somber, Kira Nerys scanned the reports on the sensor padd on the table before her at the operations station. She looked around at the other officers, people she had begun to think could do anything they put their minds to.

Somehow she didn't have that feeling today. Everyone looked vulnerable—was she imagining it?

They looked tired. She certainly wasn't imagining that part. She'd been driving them hard.

"We've run seven simulations," she said, "and they've all come up the same. The Jem'Hadar overwhelm our defenses and board the station within two hours."

Dr. Julian Bashir stood on the periphery of the command circle, his large eyes and tender expression pleated with concern. "Two hours doesn't even give us time to get reinforcements from Bajor."

"There must be something we've overlooked." Trying to sound encouraging, Jadzia Dax gave him a placating nod. Even she, the oasis of calm for all of them, couldn't drum up a convincing possibility. She stopped talking, as if she understood that they'd be better off without statements like that. Nonconstructive hope was for children.

"Major," O'Brien said finally, after everybody had looked at everybody else, "I'm the last one to say it's hopeless, but given DS9's structural limitations, our available power supply, and the difficulty of defending a stationary target against a heavily armed mobile force . . . I'd say two hours is optimistic."

Kira buried her frustration in a few passes of pacing about the Ops deck. Ultimately she turned to their head of security, the man responsible for keeping peace on this boiling speck in space.

Constable Odo looked at her, his incomplete face smooth as plastic, his demeanor cautious.

"All right," Kira began, "let's say we let them board the station. That still doesn't mean we have to surrender."

"What are you suggesting?" Dax spoke up from behind her.

"We can hide in the conduits . . . set up booby traps . . . prepare ambushes. Try to hold out until we can get reinforcements."

"We can try," Odo said, "but I don't think there would be much of a station left by the time they got here."

Taking his pronouncement stoically, Kira paced again. Odo knew more about the innards of *Deep Space Nine* than any of them. He'd simply been here longer.

Dax, as usual, absorbed the facts a little quicker than anyone else. "That leaves us with two options. Abandon the station and make a stand on Bajor, or collapse the entrance to the wormhole."

Kira turned to her. "I want a third alternative. I refuse to believe that we can't—"

Alarms broke over her words.

At the science station, Dax's beautiful eyes were fixed on her console. "Some kind of large subspace surge just activated our security sensors."

Glancing around at the other officers at their stations, Kira assured herself that everything else was stable and she could concentrate on Dax's discovery. "Where is it?"

"Bearing one four eight, mark two one five." Dax's voice was damnably calm. How the hell could she do that? "Distance, three hundred meters."

"Three hundred *meters?*" O'Brien blurted. "That's almost inside our shield perimeter!"

"From the intensity and the harmonic signature," Dax filled in, "it might be a cloaked ship, but I've never seen an energy dispersal pattern like this."

Kira gritted her teeth. Muscles knotted and

throat tight, bullied by thoughts that had driven her to the holosuites for a most unrelaxing practice, she bolted, "Could it be the Jem'Hadar?"

O'Brien almost—only almost—rolled his eyes, except that he knew it wasn't a paranoid question. "Nothing's come through the wormhole in the past two days."

"It's too close for comfort, whatever it is," Kira said. "Raise shields. Energize phaser banks. Stand by to lock—"

"The energy signature's fluctuating," Dax interrupted. "It's decloaking."

In near space before them on the main viewer, a bulky, compact space vessel wobbled out of cloak, shedding the parcel of night it had used as its mirage of nothing. It was chunky, heavily muscled, but obviously a Starfleet design and bearing Starfleet and Federation insignia. More than just familiar—it was *starship* design.

But she also knew that ships could be stolen. Who was aboard that thing?

She knew what the crew was expecting, but she refused to order shields down prematurely.

Just for the sake of hearing it, Dax mentioned, "It's definitely a Federation starship . . . but I've never seen this design."

"A Federation ship," O'Brien added, "with a cloaking device?"

Dax started to respond, then cut herself off with, "They're hailing us."

Kira nodded to her.

The screen bawbled faintly, then shifted to a

crystal-clear image of the last person they expected to see sitting in a command chair of a starship.

"Hello, Major," Commander Benjamin Sisko began, in that orchestra-pit bass-section voice. "Sorry to startle you, but I wanted to test the *Defiant*'s cloaking device."

Kira straightened. "The *Defiant?*"

On the screen, Sisko was holding back a grin. His dark brown face was rosy with satisfaction.

But his eyes were grinning.

"I've brought back a little surprise for the Dominion."

CHAPTER
2

BEN SISKO had waited all week for the looks on his stationmates' faces when he flew in with that compact gut-puncher of a starship. The *U.S.S. Defiant* didn't exactly have the water-lily elegance of starships that had come before her, but she wasn't meant for a casual swim.

He came into the observatory wardroom with a little sigh of relief at being back. The dreary, harsh room had undergone a renovation since he took over the station, but the basic architecture was still that of the original owners. The Cardassian structure was hard and chilly, barely offset by comfortable Federation lounge chairs, a couple of couches and end tables, and the big table for formal meetings. The only element that kept the room from looking like a Starfleet Headquarters guest hall was the big viewer and computer console at the far end.

Most of his officers were here waiting for him, all with their backs to the entrance, gazing down through an observation port at the docked starship, so preoccupied that none of them heard him come in.

There was Dax, standing as relaxed as a reed, O'Brien at a version of parade rest, Kira at a version of no rest at all, and Julian Bashir leaning forward the way a little boy peeks over the safety wall at the zoo's tiger den.

And standing just a few inches more than necessary away from the rest of them was Odo. Sisko noted that his security chief's thin, rangy body was a fraction thinner and rangier than the last time he'd seen him. At first, Sisko had thought he was imagining these subtle changes. Then he discovered that Odo would occasionally experiment with the human form, to see if he could get it a little more "right" today than yesterday. It was a sad but valiant effort to fit in with beings who had solid form in their natural states. He couldn't get the face right, daily dealing with children's stares at his masklike facsimile, so he tended to put extra effort into the things he could manage. To Odo, solidity would always be a mystery.

But even though he never admitted it, he was always trying.

Sisko grinned warmly and wished there were some way he could help Odo without embarrassing him.

"It's an interesting design," Dax was saying, somewhat dubiously, as they all gazed at the starship, "but there's a certain . . . inelegance to it."

Sisko almost announced himself, but when no one turned, he kept quiet. He couldn't tell if Dax was boning up to spare his feelings or not, and felt a little insulted that she would worry about that. After all, he wasn't bringing home a stray puppy he'd fallen in love with.

So why was he standing here, eavesdropping?

"Inelegant's a polite way of putting it," O'Brien said. "I'd call her ugly."

"I don't know." The mellow offer of Dr. Bashir from beside O'Brien, that wistful English this-won't-hurt-a-bit tone, helped more than Sisko wanted to admit. "I think there's a somewhat romantic quality to her. Almost heroic."

Smiling at that, Sisko moved up behind them. "I'm afraid there's nothing romantic or heroic about her, Doctor."

They all turned at once, looking like children who'd been caught getting into the Halloween candy one day early. He came forward among them, looked out the window, then fed a computer cartridge into the nearest monitor and keyed it in.

Silently a schematic of the ship from the top and both sides popped onto a small screen. He didn't have to tell his crew to take a look. They were already crowded around him.

"Officially she's classified as an escort vessel. Unofficially, the *Defiant*'s a warship. Nothing more, nothing less."

"I thought Starfleet didn't believe in warships," Kira baited, taking a little poke with her tone.

"Desperate times breed desperate measures," Sisko admitted.

It had never been his venue to protect the Federation's long- or shortsightedness, and he wasn't inclined to start now.

"Five years ago, Starfleet began exploring the possibility of building a new class of starship—a Federation battle cruiser. This ship would have no families, no science labs, no luxuries of any kind. It would be designed for one purpose only—to fight and defeat the Borg."

He drew a breath and held it for a beat. Was he keeping the lingering ache out of his voice? The gut-gnawing images of his wife's body lying in the crumpled rubble after the Borg attack, of his son's racking sobs as he told the boy he couldn't see his mommy anymore.

"The *Defiant*," he pushed forward, "was the prototype. The first ship in what might have been a new Federation battle fleet."

"But the threat from the Borg receded," Dax took over, "so Starfleet never pursued the project."

He nodded in confirmation, but also in gratitude. He knew she'd caught the warble of emotion in his voice and wanted to give him a chance to catch it back.

After clearing his throat just enough, he said, "Exactly. That, combined with certain design flaws discovered during the ship's initial testing period, was enough to convince Starfleet to abandon the project."

"What sort of 'design' flaws?" O'Brien asked. For the first time he took his eyes off the dense, obsessive bruiser hanging there at the dock.

"You'll have complete access to the ship evaluation reports, Chief, but to put it simply, it's overgunned and overpowered for a ship its size. During battle drills, the ship almost tore itself apart when the engines were tested at full capacity."

Kira angled toward him. "And *this* is the ship Starfleet sent us to fight the Dominion?"

Suddenly Sisko felt defensive again, wanting to throw ice on the underlying sentiment behind her words—that the Bajorans, their planet, and the station orbiting it had come in last again on Starfleet's priority roster.

He empathized with Kira. The one thing she did believe in would be a warship. There was no one faster to take up arms in the defense of freedom than someone who had not always enjoyed it.

"We're not going to *fight* the Dominion, Major," he said. "At least, not yet."

He moved around the table. Like students tagging behind a teacher, they followed him.

"Our mission," he went on, "is to take the *Defiant* into the Gamma Quadrant and try to find the leaders of the Dominion—the Founders. We have to convince them that the Federation represents no threat to them."

He didn't add, and hoped they would all just figure out for themselves, that the Federation could do that anytime it wanted. The subliminal reason for taking a power-packed starship was to communicate to the Dominion that, while the Federation posed no threat, it was ready and able to threaten if pushed to do so.

He also understood the foolhardiness of what he was planning, of going into space where they had been attacked en masse, where a Galaxy-class starship had been blown to glitters. As tactics went, the next step in avoiding war had to be this show-no-fear negotiation. Many an ambassador had never returned from this kind of mission.

All he could do was hedge his bet and take the first step. He was going in as an ambassador with a white flag in one hand and a whip in the other.

"But sir," Bashir quietly asked, "what if they just don't believe us?"

Oh, well. So much for keeping everything interiorized. Sisko turned to him. "That's why I asked for the *Defiant*. She may have flaws, but she has *teeth*. I want the Dominion to know that we *can* and *will* defend ourselves if necessary."

Kira didn't look convinced, but she didn't argue. That meant she understood that he'd made his decision and it would stand for now.

"Computer," Sisko began, "show me a tactical representation of the Gamma Quadrant, highlighting the known areas of Dominion activity."

The monitor brightened with a star chart, clearly showing the mouth of the wormhole that connected them to the far-distant Gamma Quadrant, but it was the mouth on the other side from them. A ten-minute ride . . . a seventy-thousand-light-year leap. Sixty-seven years on the fastest Federation starship.

There were several areas on the chart labeled "Dominion." Each carried a disturbing mystery. Sisko pointed to the nearest one.

"We'll begin here. With the Karemma. From what we know, the Karemma evidently joined the

Dominion peacefully and of their own accord. They've set up a trading agreement with the Ferengi, so they're used to dealing with people from the Alpha Quadrant."

"And you think they'll lead us to the Founders?" Dax anticipated.

Unwilling to commit quite that much sureness, Sisko said, "I think they're a good place to start."

He started to explain more, probably more than he should have, but that was moot when the entrance door whispered open and a Starfleet security man came in, along with a less likely character—a female Romulan in officer's clothing.

Around him, his crew instinctively stiffened up at the presence of this habitual enemy. They weren't making any aggressive moves, but they were ready to take their cues from him. As such, he was careful what movements he made.

While the Romulan lingered back, the security man came straight to Sisko. "I've posted two security officers at the *Defiant*'s docking port, sir. No one'll get near the cloaking device without us knowing about it."

For the first time, now that the subject had slipped into his parlor, Odo spoke up in that gravelly tone just short of accusation. "I wasn't informed about any special security needs."

The Romulan woman tilted in. "The security arrangements were made at my request. To protect the cloaking device."

Risking life, limb, future, and his ability to stand upright without wincing, Sisko stepped between them. "A few introductions are in order. This is

Subcommander T'Rul of the Romulan Empire. She is here to operate the cloaking device which her government has so kindly lent us for this mission."

He was trying to be nice without being too nice. There hadn't exactly been a peace agreement between the Federation and the Romulan Empire—more like a tacit pause—but the Romulans weren't so puffed up with themselves that they couldn't see the advantage in holding back the invasion of some new force from the other side of the wormhole before they'd gotten advantage on this side.

At least Sisko hoped that was the logic. He wasn't a diplomat and hadn't been in on those meetings, so he just decided what was best for his station and the planet he protected, and hoped he was right about motivations of others.

T'Rul's expression wasn't giving anything away. "Romulan interests," she said, "will be served by cooperation. And my role is to keep 'unauthorized personnel' away from the cloaking device."

Well, that was it. She'd managed to sweep every one of the station people into one gaze and make sure they knew she wasn't just referring to the odd tourist's curiosity. She meant them, uniforms or not.

Sisko turned so that his shoulder was slightly between her and his people. "May I present my officers . . . this is Major Kira Nerys—"

"Thank you, but I know their names," T'Rul said. "And I'm not here to make friends."

She spun on a heel and went out the exit. The door as it shut seemed to breathe *And she knows how to make enemies.*

23

"Charming," Kira grumbled.

The security man pushed toward her, with his hand out. "Well, I *am* here to make friends. I'm Lieutenant Commander Paul Eddington, Starfleet Security."

Kira took his hand and obviously battled for civility. "Major Kira Nerys."

"Lieutenant Jadzia Dax," Dax said as he turned to her.

O'Brien was still catching glimpses of that ship, but stopped in time to add, "Chief Miles O'Brien."

Bashir, though, was all hospitality as he caught Eddington's hand and pumped it. "Dr. Julian Bashir."

Eddington smiled and nodded, then turned to Odo and almost stuck his hand toward him, but caught the chilly glare from that plastic face and didn't insist.

"Odo. Head of *station* security," Odo said, bristling. "May I ask what your function is here, Commander?"

Eddington looked surprised. He glanced at Sisko, realizing he had somehow compromised him.

Watching Odo's displeasure deepen, Sisko steeled to avoid what he least looked forward to doing. Maybe he could put it off. "There's to be a complete mission briefing at eighteen hundred hours, but be prepared to depart the station at oh-seven-hundred. Dismissed."

Dax led the way out; Kira frowned, then followed. O'Brien almost knocked the two women down in his dive below to get at the guts of that ship, and Bashir disappeared in the other direction down the corridor with only one glance back, then looked at Eddington, who was following him, also glad to get out of there.

The door closed with a breathy *whup.*

Sisko looked wantingly after them, wishing he could get out of this.

Funny how much indignation could show through that smooth, featureless face of Odo's. Maybe it was all in the eyes.

"You needn't brace yourself to give me unpleasant news, Commander," Odo said. "I'll save you the trouble. I've been relieved as chief of security."

He turned in studious unceremony and angled out of the wardroom.

That was Odo . . . no ceremony. Blunt. Yes, no, up, down. No middle.

Sisko hurried after him—and it was work to catch up.

"Odo—wait."

Perhaps he accidentally slipped a tacit *That's an order* into his voice, because Odo stopped.

Sisko pulled up short. He'd been gearing for a long run down the corridor.

"You have *not* been relieved," he contradicted. "You will continue to be in charge of internal security aboard the station. On the Promenade, your word is law. You answer to no one except me. You're still in charge of all non-Starfleet security matters aboard this station."

"And what about *off* the Promenade? What about matters that *are* Starfleet?"

"In those areas, you'll have to coordinate your efforts with Lieutenant Commander Eddington."

Only as he said it did Sisko realize the mistake he'd made in flashing Eddington's full rank again before Odo. It sounded so authoritarian—

"'Coordinate' is another way of saying I'll report to him," Odo interpreted coldly.

Sisko lowered his voice. "I'm sorry, Odo. This wasn't my idea."

"I'm sure it wasn't. You're just . . . following orders."

Now Sisko raised his voice again, since lowering it hadn't done a bit of good. "An idea I strongly disagree with. I did everything I could to fight this. I even took it to the chief of Starfleet Security herself."

"May I ask why so much effort was required to keep me here?"

Feeling like he'd been punched with that one—a painfully good question—Sisko struggled, "There was a concern . . . regarding several recent security breaches."

"If I had been given the authority I asked for," Odo bristled, "instead of being tied to Starfleet regulations, there wouldn't have been any security breaches."

"Odo, your resistance to following Starfleet regulations is part of the problem."

"I think there might be a simpler explanation, Commander. Starfleet decided to bring in someone they could trust," Odo said bluntly. "Someone besides 'the shapeshifter.'"

"This isn't a racial issue, Odo," Sisko surfeited, even though he knew his steady, dependable, long-time and always alien officer had another good point, like it or not. "I understand and I want you to know——"

"You needn't bother, Commander," Odo said. No matter his stance or his expression, he couldn't dispatch the insult or the regret from what he was saying. "I don't require your understanding. My resignation will be logged within the hour."

"Constable! Constable, a moment of your time, please! Odo, wait!"

Quark had caught a glimpse of Odo skimming past the bar entrance and almost tripped on a spilled drink trying to get out there before the constable reverted to his natural state and seeped into a doorjamb or something.

He called one more time, and Odo finally stopped and turned, a bitter no-kidding look on his—well, face.

"What is it, Quark?" the shapeshifter drawled, letting the Ferengi know that he was the last person on Odo's list of guests for teatime right now.

Quark pulled up quickly and kept a wide step between himself and that expression.

"I just wanted to see if . . . it's true."

Brooding, Odo held himself stiff. "If that's your way of asking if I've been relieved, then the answer is yes. I'm sure that makes you very happy, so now I'll stand here and patiently wait for you to finish gloating."

At Odo's "laugh if you want to" posture, Quark plowed through the shiver of guilt that would make Odo feel this way, admitting to himself that their relationship had gone beyond just that of a shady dealer and a beat cop.

"I'm not here to gloat," he said. His lips weren't even twitching.

"Then if you'll excuse me." Odo turned to go.

Quark fell in step a little behind him. "What happened?" he persisted.

"Starfleet has sent their own security officer. A Lieutenant Commander Eddington. He'll be in charge as of this afternoon."

"A Starfleet officer?" Quark echoed. "But why? How did this happen? What does Commander Sisko say about this?"

Odo stopped so sharply that Quark had to duck the constable's shoulder as he spun around.

"Why are you so concerned?" Odo said. "After all, you'll have a brand-new security chief to deal with. One that's not as familiar with you and your venal ways. You should be celebrating, Quark. Victory is yours."

For a flash, Quark almost admitted that Odo was right, but that for some reason he still didn't like the idea of a change. He knew how much the job meant to Odo, that it was everything to Odo— purpose, anchorage, self-value—even the family Odo had never found he had found here.

Desperate that he might be found stumbling over sentiment, and knowing Odo would recoil from that, Quark forced a snarling grin and connived to make Odo feel successful.

"On the contrary," Quark attempted, "this upsets my entire operation."

"How so?"

"You were good," Quark offered, spinning the yarn as he went. "You kept me on my lobes. You made sure I didn't get lazy and careless. Beating you made me better."

He paused and waited. That wasn't bad. Hey— maybe he could polish this and build it into a technique. Adding a touch of underlying honesty . . . not bad at all.

He wished he could keep better control, though.

Odo peered at him from inside the buffed mask of human skin. "You never beat me," he said.

The mood of banter the two could usually raise wilted abruptly. Odo turned and strode off, cool as open space.

Quark gazed after him. Sadness washed the smug light of success off his face.

"If you say so," he murmured.

Ben Sisko plunged into his own quarters with a full cache of relief in both hands. Here was the only place where he wasn't the commander of the station, attendant of a planet, and guardian of a bridge between quadrants.

Here, he was just Dad.

And custodian of an incredible mess.

All around the quarters, suitcases were opened and partially emptied, clothing that had been on its way to drawers dumped over the arms of furniture instead, and a shipping crate sitting untended in the middle of the floor.

And a boy, lanky as pampas grass, looking up at him and guiltily cradling a bowl of spice pudding. The spoon was still in his mouth.

Sisko frowned. "I thought you were unpacking."

Jake Sisko's eyes were big as the scoops of pudding he'd been enjoying. "I am! I mean, I was. But I just kept looking at the replicator and thinking . . . and . . ."

"And you just had to have some I'danian spice pudding."

"I still can't believe we couldn't find a decent bowl of it back on Earth!"

Glad to be dealing with something other than that look of betrayal in Odo's eyes, Sisko smiled. "That didn't stop you from ordering it from every replicator you saw."

He started unpacking, turning just enough to give Jake the chance to heap another spoonful into his mouth.

The utilitarian duties of unpacking should've been therapeutic, but instead they only reminded him that he had never unpacked his own clothes before his wife died. Jennifer had always done that. She'd always liked it.

He didn't like it so well.

"So is it good to be home?" he asked his son.

"Yeah," the teenager said quickly. "I can't wait to sleep in my own bed again."

Sisko stopped what he was doing, hovering there with a handful of clothing. "I wonder when that happened. . . ."

Jake turned. "What?"

Looking around the room in wonder and just a touch of shock, Sisko flopped into a chair. "When did it happen? When did I start thinking of this Cardassian monstrosity as . . . home?"

Jake smiled. "I think it happened last Thursday. Around seventeen hundred hours." Pretending to be suave and mysterious, the boy went to the big crate and opened it. "When you took all this stuff out of storage down on Earth."

He reached inside and pulled out an intricately carved wooden mask, and waggled it dramatically.

Sisko bounded from his chair and caught the mask. "Careful! That's a two-thousand-year-old Yoruba mask. And that 'stuff' is one of the finest collections of ancient—"

" '—of ancient African art you'll ever see.' I know," Jake said. "And I also know how much it means to you. But to me, it was always the 'stuff' in your library. At *home*. When you took it out of storage so you could bring it here, it meant Earth wasn't home anymore. This was."

Sisko gazed at his son, and realized as if for the first time that they were looking eye-to-eye at each other. Jake was as tall as he was. Something deep inside protested and wanted to rush into the other room and invent a shrink-beam.

But it wasn't just Jake's height that was grown-up anymore. For a while, that had been all. Now there was more.

For one thing, the boy—the young man—didn't look away or flinch at his father's direct glare.

That was new too.

Sisko broke the gaze and reached into the box. His hand actually cooled as he reached in. The box had sat a long time in storage.

He pulled out a statue of a naked human form, made of polished dark wood and elongated to enhance the mythical. After some consideration, he selected a spot in the room to display it . . . where the soft lights would caress the hips and shoulders.

"What do you think?" he asked.

Jake stood back and surveyed the mask, charging this item as the first confirmation of this floating alien perch as their permanent lodging. Their home.

"Perfect," he said.

The stars could be beautiful sometimes. To Kira, they had always meant a measure of safety, or a chance to escape, hide, or attack. She had only come to see them as pretty in the past couple of years, and only through the eyes of these humans who came to help guard her planet from its age-old enemies.

The Earth people had poems about stars and the night, songs about them, and they talked about them to their lovers.

It had taken some time to shake the underground soldier out of herself enough to just look at the stars for what they were, little winks of light set in a distant matte, and not take them as a signal in the deadly gloom.

After peeking in the doors of two dozen possible places to be alone on DS9, she found Odo at one of the observation windows, staring out at those stars.

What could they mean to him?

She paused behind him for a few seconds, and looked out there, then looked at the way he was looking at them.

There wasn't a clue in his posture—only the stillness of it.

"Odo, there you are," she said finally, pretending to just walk up. And she knew he'd heard her coming. "I've just finished talking to the provisional government. They want you to go with us to the Gamma Quadrant tomorrow as an official Bajoran representative."

"I'm no diplomat," he snapped back, as though closing a lid.

She pulled up beside him and tried to relax her shoulders, to act as if all this hadn't been so contrived that it smelled of glue. "I know. That's why they want you to go. If we do find the Founders, we'll need more than just diplomacy. We'll need to size them up as a security risk . . . see what kind of threat they really pose to Bajor. Analyze their—"

"You're the military expert, Major," he droned, "not me. And I doubt that the provisional government contacted you and asked for my presence in any capacity on this mission." He paused. His tone changed for the better, but not the less painful. "If I'm not mistaken, this is simply a somewhat misguided effort to . . . make me feel better."

Feeling like either a bad liar or a miserable actress, Kira dropped the pretense. "Maybe it is," she said. "Maybe I'm your friend. And maybe I want you to see that you're still needed here, regardless of what some idiot Starfleet admiral might think. But I also want you on this mission because I think we'll need you."

His eyes moved inside that formless face, but he didn't turn to her.

Pushing the point, she went on. "Odo, we're taking an untried ship into what may be a combat situation. There's a Romulan officer aboard . . . who knows what else is going to pop up in our faces."

He kept looking out the window. Said nothing.

Kira waited, realizing that the ultimatum might have been too much.

He still wasn't talking. He hadn't jumped on the idea of helping her, no matter how pathetic or desperate she'd tried to sound. She hoped she didn't sound *too* pathetic.

But he wasn't saying he *wouldn't* go either, was he?

She backed away from him, moving just slightly toward the exit, so he would know he wasn't going to be pressured any more.

"The *Defiant* leaves at seven hundred hours," she said.

When she left, he was still looking out the window.

CHAPTER
3

SISKO FOUND HIS OFFICE a little too clean and a little too cool after having been unoccupied for so long, but was glad to be conducting business here and not in some office at Starfleet Headquarters, where all the advantages belonged to somebody else.

Before him, twitching, puzzled, and nervous, Quark was holding his hands down at the sides of his chair and trying not to panic.

Sisko just waited it out and let his request sink it.

"I'm a little confused, Commander," Quark began, trying to frame his question cautiously. "You want *me* to go with *you* to the Gamma Quadrant? To help you find the Founders?"

"See?" Sisko slapped his knee. "It's not so confusing after all."

Quark's brow ridge drooped and he stared at Sisko as if wondering when the laughter was coming. "You . . . you're joking with me, aren't you? Having a little fun with Quark?" He smiled and tried to hedge the conversation with a nervous laugh.

"I'm quite serious."

"You can't be!" The smile evaporated. "I'm not a diplomat, or an explorer, or a tactical officer, or whatever else you might need on this trip! Now, if you need a caterer, I'll be happy to send a new replicator that I just got from—"

"Eight months ago, you helped the Nagus establish a trade agreement with the Karemma. Tulaberry wine, I believe. The Karemma are part of the Dominion."

"A minor part—a very minor part."

"They still may be able to help us contact the Founders. Since you're experienced in dealing with the Karemma, you seem like a logical person to—"

"Actually," Quark burped, "my brother Rom did most of the talking. I think he would be better-suited for this mission."

"Not Rom," Sisko said evenly. "You."

"But why? Rom only has a child to think about! I have a business to run!"

"You," Sisko repeated. He was determined to hedge every bet he was making, no matter how much whining he had to field.

Quark stood up abruptly and edged toward the door. "I'm sorry, Commander, but I must refuse. My last experience with the Jem'Hadar was not a pleasant one and I don't intend to repeat it. Now, there's no way you can legally force me to—"

A loud *crack* sounded through the office as force met immutable object—a cane across Sisko's desk.

It had the desired effect on Quark, who hit the office ceiling and the ceiling in the room above them. Shivering, he turned and saw that Sisko was cradling an ornate stick whose significance they both understood.

"The scepter of the Grand Nagus!" Quark gasped, still wincing from the sound.

"I had a chance to discuss this mission with him on my way back from Earth," Sisko calmly explained, with more than just a little bit of double entendre slobbered into every key word. "He seemed to agree with me that unless peaceful contact is established with the Founders, business opportunities in the Gamma Quadrant might suddenly dry up." He caressed the cane, but never took his eyes off Quark. "He also agreed that you were the perfect man to help me."

"I don't believe it," Quark spat, his small body quaking now.

"Which . . . is why he sent this along," Sisko continued. "He thought it might convince you of the high value he places on the success of this mission."

He extended the cane, pointing the carved Ferengi face on the pommel directly at Quark as if the little nasty expression were looking right at him.

"Now," he said, "are you going to defy the wishes of the Grand Nagus himself?"

Managing a pained excuse for a smile, Quark stared into the batlike face on the end of the cane.

Sisko held it as still as he could. He wanted those little vicious wooden eyes boring right through Quark's natural cowardice.

"No," Quark said, shivering again. "No, of course not . . . I'm . . . happy to serve the Nagus . . . and you in any way I can."

Withdrawing the cane but not putting it down, Sisko said, "Thank you, Quark. I knew I could count on you."

Quark looked as if his legs had turned to putty as he shuffled toward the exit.

"Quark?" Sisko held the cane out again. "Aren't you forgetting something?"

Knowing Sisko was making the last twist, and that he couldn't get out of his own nation's requirements, at least not in front of an audience, Quark reluctantly moved back in and kissed the wooden Ferengi head.

"Benjamin, may I come in?"

Sisko looked up from the Grand Nagus's cane. How long had he been staring at it?

"You didn't answer your door chime," Jadzia Dax said as she willowed into his office and made herself comfortable in the chair on the other side of his desk, "so I just barged in."

"I guess I wasn't paying attention," he said sullenly.

Her long lovely face and dark back-combed hair pulled back and tied studiously were framed by the mineral colors of the wall behind her. "You didn't ask for my report in front of the others. I took that as a signal that you didn't want anything spread around yet."

With a glance he thanked her and confirmed that at the same time. "Complete evacuation is worked out, then?"

"Yes."

"Who knows about it?"

"No one, except the captain of the transport. I made all the arrangements myself. Even our shuttle pilots don't know the purpose of their standbys. The minute the Jem'Hadar poke their noses through the wormhole, all children and nonessential station residents and personnel will be loaded onto shuttles and runabouts and taken to a secluded prearranged spot on the Bajoran arctic, where there's a large warp-speed transport sitting in readiness to remand them to Federation custody on Camus II. It's all set up, but it's very unofficial at the moment."

"How did you do that without telling anybody?" he asked.

Lifting one shoulder in a docile shrug, she condensed, "I programmed computer recognition signals to process in a domino effect. The right people will be notified step by step, but not ahead of time. There's a certain risk—"

"But I'll take it." Sisko dismissed the subject with a shrug of his own, then found himself thinking about it anyway. "If the Jem'Hadar get a whiff of an evacuation plan, they'll take it as a sign of weakness and an invitation to attack."

She nodded. "You might like to know that the *Defiant* will be ready at oh-seven-hundred hours."

"Did it pass the chief's inspection?"

"Does anything? He has a maintenance list about as long as this table, but he said it'll get us where we're going."

"And back, I hope."

"He said that was up to you."

Sisko smiled, and sat on the edge of the desk. The smile faded.

"I'd never have volunteered for this mission unless I thought we had a chance of coming back," he thought aloud.

"You *volunteered,*" Dax harassed. "How many times did Curzon tell you never to volunteer for anything?"

Sisko gazed at her, lost for a moment.

God, she looked young! How old was the life-force inside her—three hundred?

Every time he turned around he still expected to see the old man he'd been used to, the codger who'd gone through Sisko's professional life with him. The oldest friend he had.

A three-hundred-year-old entity, there in the body of a twenty-seven-year-old beauty.

She had always said she was still Curzon Dax inside, but he couldn't quite buy that. Something of Curzon was gone and something of Jadzia was here, and tolerance notwithstanding it just wasn't normal for people to swap bodies.

"As I recall," he said, "Curzon broke that rule a few times himself."

"And regretted it every time."

"This is different. I'd end up regretting it more if

we just sat around here and waited for an invasion."

Dax moved around the desk. "If I know Starfleet, they must've run about two hundred probability studies on this mission of ours. What are the odds we succeed?"

"Slim. But better than the odds of fighting off a Jem'Hadar assault on the station." He slid off the desk and paced. "And if the station falls . . . Bajor falls. And I will *not* let that happen."

Dax watched him for several seconds, giving him no hints about what she was thinking, or remembering. She let him sweat for a long time, until he was stirred with curiosity and ready to beg her to say what she had in mind.

"You know," she said, obviously anticipating him, "after Jennifer died, I never thought I'd see you so passionate about something."

"Until two months ago, I would've agreed with you. Then I went back to Earth and I spent all those weeks being debriefed at Starfleet Headquarters . . . I used to get a thrill just walking into that building. I used to look around at the admirals and think, One day that's going to be me. One day I'm going to be the one making the big decisions."

"Curzon used to think that was very funny," she said.

He frowned at her. "Did he?"

"What I mean is, he could never see a set of admiral's stars on your shoulder. He thought that just *making* decisions would never satisfy you. You had to implement them. See the results. Face the consequences. Curzon always thought you were the kind of man who has to be in the thick of things . . . not sitting behind a desk at headquarters."

Sisko gave in to a reserved grin, baffled at the way she talked about her previous "self" as if he were a deceased uncle. They both knew it wasn't exactly that way.

"He was a very smart old man, wasn't he?"

She tilted her head. "He liked to think so."

"You'd better get some sleep," he said.

"I was about to say the same thing to you. See you in the morning, Benjamin."

"Yes . . . I guess there's nothing more to do than get one last good night's sleep before we take that ship out," he said. "We'll be operating with a skeleton crew. We won't get much rest."

"That's all right. The *Defiant* certainly is encouraging to the crew," she offered, trying to pass the encouragement along to him. "Kira and O'Brien have been crawling around aboard her half the night. It's giving fuel to the gossip."

Sisko looked up. "What gossip?"

Her black eyelashes cast shadows on her cheeks as she batted them with silly drama. "The two of them have been spending a lot of time in Quark's holosuites while you've been gone."

"The two of them?" Sisko sputtered. "Kira and O'Brien?"

"Almost every day."

"That's . . . outlandish! O'Brien's the most married man I—"

Halfway through the phrase he caught the sparkle

42

in her eyes and knew he was being had. The holosuites.

"Oh . . . Kira. Battle simulations. Right?"

Dax grinned a nasty satisfaction that didn't go with the Helen of Troy image. "Well, the gossip's fun anyway."

Uncomforted, Sisko dropped back into his chair and let it rock.

"Kira doesn't trust me," he sadly proclaimed.

Dax shook her head and blasted him with a harsh expression. "Benjamin!"

"She doesn't think I'll put Bajor far enough forward in my defense plans. She's my second-in-command, but she sees herself as the first defender of her home planet. She's looking for ways to protect the planet herself if she has to. Let's face it—that's why she's cooperating with Starfleet in the first place."

"I honestly don't think that's true at all."

"I do," he said. "It's what I would do." When she didn't say anything, he sighed and kept pulling the same string. "How will everyone on Bajor react when they find out about an evacuation plan? They'll see Federation betrayal before their very eyes. We'll be emptying *Deep Space Nine,* Federation personnel pouring out of the sector, and the people on Bajor will be left behind. If it comes down to that, I'll have to do that no matter how I feel about it. Is that the kind of membership we've been promising these people? We can't evacuate a whole planet, can we?"

Again Dax didn't say anything.

"As of today," Sisko went on, "there's a good

chance that Jake will be evacuated to Bajor, then moved to safety, and all the Bajoran children still planetside will be sitting ducks."

"Possibly," Dax warranted, "but how would Jake's death on a bombed-out station help them? You have to give yourself an inch, Benjamin."

Sisko knew he sounded as if he were feeling sorry for himself, and he would be forever grateful that she didn't point that out.

"What kind of father am I?" he said. "I wanted to run away after Jennifer died, but I knew I had to raise my son. So I ran halfway away . . . to *Deep Space Nine*. And now look what I've given him."

She didn't seem moved by that. "Pioneers have been taking children with them for thousands of years. Safety isn't the reason to live life. We take it when we can get it, but we should never give up too much for it. After all, if the Jem'Hadar are successful, do you think he'll be that much safer on Earth?"

Sisko leered at her and allowed himself a whipped smile. "I could always count on you for the brutal truth. And why does that terrible image make me feel better?"

Dax nodded a silent and sarcastic you're-welcome, teasing him with her underlying complexity.

"I hear you've asked Quark to come along on the *Defiant* mission," she said, trying to crank the conversation in another direction.

A bitter chuckle jumped in his chest. "I didn't 'ask' him. I scared him." He tapped the cane against his palm.

Dax looked as if she just couldn't get the reaction she wanted today.

"It couldn't have been that bad," she said. "Quark's not that hard to scare."

"He really didn't want to go." Sisko leaned back and his chair reclined accommodatingly. "You know, I was *this* close to letting him off the hook. If he'd resisted another two seconds, I'd have let him off. If he'd known how close I was, he'd have pressed for his rights to stay." He shook the cane in the air between them. "I distracted him."

She didn't exactly smile, but it was under there. "Did you take a self-pity seminar while you were gone?"

"You know why. It's one thing to ask Starfleet personnel to put their lives on the line. It's something else to ask a civilian resident of the station. Quark didn't want to go. He can't be forced by law. He doesn't *have* to go. I made him go. You should've seen it—it was plain coercion. If this works out, I swear I'll *stand* on the Grand Nagus if I have to, to get Quark what he wants from the Gamma Quadrant."

He fell to uneasy silence, still swiveling in his chair as though he were blowing in the wind.

Dax kept looking at him with that little pucker of a smile.

He sighed and picked at a fingernail. "I feel like a puppy who just missed the boat."

Dax's smile broke as she laughed at him. "No mixing metaphors on duty. So far this mission is successful. You brought us a starship, you got Starfleet Security to assign us a team—"

"That wasn't what I wanted!" He flared his hands in frustration. "Not the way they gave it to me. What am I going to do about Odo? I don't want him to quit. He understands this station—"

"But he doesn't understand that you understated your confrontation with Starfleet, I'll bet," Dax said.

Again, she had him. He glowered at her. "What is it with those people? I *think* I was speaking English . . . the more I asked for additional security, the more they interpreted it as if the security that's already here isn't good enough. They didn't seem to be hearing the ends of any of my sentences. Those pointy-headed desk jockeys have no idea how much trouble can occur on a station this far out, or how well Odo has managed to deflect most of it. And I can't even tell him how hard I fought for him."

"No, you can't," she confirmed. "It would only substantiate what he already thinks . . . that Starfleet would rather he weren't around."

"Yes, well," he grumbled, "after some of the language I used, they're going to take back the 'gentleman' part of my 'officer and a gentleman' title."

Stiffly, he pulled the chair around and got up, gnashing his way about the office to burn off some of this aggravation.

Dax sat solemn as a nun and watched him go back and forth.

Finally she said, "Benjamin, will you tell me what happened at Starfleet Headquarters or am I going to have to hire a psychic?"

"I just told you."

"You told me about Quark and Odo and Jake and Bajor. That's not what's really at the bottom of this mood."

She shifted her shoulders against the chair, crossed her ankles, and settled back as if she intended not to leave until she pried this rock off him.

Sisko swashed back and forth before the office viewing monitors, each of which showed a different part of the station—the Promenade, the airlock corridors, the habitat ring—and people moving about casually on each, occasionally somebody running to meet a schedule.

"What went on at headquarters," he echoed. "Arguments, that's what. Some people wanted to commit half the Fleet to guarding the wormhole. That's what *I* wanted. The Jem'Hadar might pack a punch, but there's only one bridge to come across. The massed power of Starfleet is hard to bet against when they can concentrate on one spot and not a whole frontier."

"I completely agree," she said. "How can anyone disagree?"

"Oh!" He shook his head and choked out a bitter noise. "There are plenty of head-in-the-sand types . . . don't build up, don't provoke, don't interfere, keep to ourselves and the Jem'Hadar will go away. . . ."

Dax clasped her hands and settled deeper into the chair. "The Jem'Hadar aren't going to go away."

"I know that. One of the Bajoran delegates even suggested blowing up the wormhole."

"Sacrificing Bajor's economic future?"

"Better than no future at all," Sisko chafed. "I couldn't blame him. They acted as if both he and I were crazy . . . overreacting."

He turned toward her with an entreating hand extended, and got another one of those little shocks. For an instant he had been talking to Curzon—the same vocal inflections, the same logic, the same manner of egging him on through his thoughts.

And there was Jadzia Dax looking back at him, gorgeous, settled, placid—what was a normal, healthy human male supposed to do when his oldest pal suddenly changed into an incredibly beautiful female?

She saw the look and her mouth turned up into the Cupid's bow again. "I'd tell you if I thought you were overreacting, Benjamin."

He looked away from her. He didn't feel like being patronized, or even tolerated.

Evidently she saw that. He could tell, because her tone changed and so did her method.

"Benjamin," she said assuringly, "in my experience, you're the one who's right. The Founders know how this game will be played. Even as far away as the Gamma Quadrant, some basic tactics will always serve. The Federation is expected to send its best fighting machine and its best people. The Jem'Hadar can either back down and be impressed, talk, or not. If not, then—"

"Then the ship *must* stand up to them." Sisko knotted his palms and butted the knuckles together. "We dare not lose. This can't be a repeat of the incident with the *Starship Odyssey*. Two minutes, and *whoosh*. Gone. If they come in and wipe the floor with us again, it's an open invitation to invade. We'll be saying, 'Here's our best, come on in, the rest is yours for the taking.' "

She nodded, then tipped her head thoughtfully. "If the strength of the Federation remains a mystery, they may not invade."

"But this will end the mystery," he said. "Our best ship. If we fail, the chance of invasion goes way up. Damned if we do and damned if we don't. Key word . . . *damned.*"

Dax watched him, but this time said nothing. Sisko realized she was walking the fine line between confidant and officer, and anything she said might be misinterpreted as strategical advice.

She was doing him the favor of sitting and listening while he talked himself into what he had to do.

"I have to go along with the Starfleet plan," he continued, "but it's not enough. It's all they would let me do. In an explosive situation, I'm being allowed to throw a match and see what happens. One ship was all they would give me, so I took it."

She didn't say anything.

He might as well have been talking to himself. She wasn't about to argue with him, and he knew she would if there was a reason to.

Sometimes it was rotten to be right.

A terrible guilt plied him suddenly. He turned his back on the wall and dropped against it, staring at the carpet.

"I should be thinking about Bajor, but I keep

thinking of Earth. The seat of the Federation, the place where I was born and raised, a wonderful place—wonderful! . . . What would Earth be like if the Jem'Hadar get through? And the colonies? The Rigel system? And all the populated Federation planets that have enjoyed freedom for so long—gone? You don't think they'll stop with Bajor, do you?"

"No, I don't," she agreed. "No one does."

"No one, but I still failed to convince the Federation how dangerous this is, and now I'm going to take one ship and make sure it's *really* dangerous. But . . . I don't know what else to do." He settled back in his chair again, not as relaxed as his posture implied. "What if we're simply overmatched this time, Dax?"

She paused at the blunt possibility. "I don't know," she said. "Can we even imagine the whole Federation turned into an occupation?"

"Why don't you say it straight out?" he incited, glaring at her. "A slave camp! Life never the same again. *Never* the same. Freedom over with. All because Ben Sisko failed to convince Starfleet to defend one little hole in space. Life would never be the same for anyone, and my son will have to live with knowing that it was his father's fault."

"Benjamin, you're carrying this too far."

"No, I'm not. Earth enslaved," he simmered. "You're right—I can't imagine it . . . but the Bajorans can. They're sitting on the line of scrimmage and I'm preoccupied with my own roots. I thought I was better than that."

"Benjamin, that's enough." She glowered expertly at him, and when he started to speak again she put out one hand, sharply, without a flinch. "No— enough. If you keep up this kind of talk, I'm not going to let you go on any more outings. I'll make you stay in your room and write a hundred times on the mirror, 'I will never again talk to Starfleet on an empty stomach.'"

Cut off in the middle of a thought, Sisko tried to keep up the self-scolding, but all at once felt a smile coming on. He tried to beat it down, but couldn't, not with her gazing at him down her nose and waiting with that hand still between them.

She'd done it. She'd broken his quarrel with himself.

His eyelids sagged dramatically as he peered at her sideways. "I'd like to see you try, skinny."

Dax marked the end of this solemn session by standing up and wandering pliantly around his office, running her finger along the edge of his desk, and finally facing him when she was within a few steps of the door.

"I think you're doing the best thing," she said amenably. "At least you have the nerve to put your hand in the fire. Since humans came out into space, you've always preached the wisdom of freedom and free association and it's always worked. No one has ever conquered the Federation and the Federation has continually expanded for over two centuries without ever having to conquer anyone else. It's unheard of in the neighboring empires. The Federation has never had to raise a weapon to force a member to join. You've just held out your hand and said, 'Join if you like.' That's what you feel you have to defend. That's what's working inside you, not whether you've said the right things to Odo or Quark or Kira or Starfleet, so don't worry about us. And the Jem'Hadar, and even the Founders, will find out in their own time what the rest of us already know."

CHAPTER
4

THE BRIDGE OF THE *Defiant* was a typical stripped-down battle bridge, like any on modern starships, but with a roughness about it. Sisko strolled around it in the early hours of morning—morning in space . . . only a relative idea. But everything, everywhere, had to run on a schedule, and even if they called the parts of the day "red," "blue," and "yellow," they would still be morning, noon, and night. Slang could come and go, but natural concepts were usually just plain sensible.

The chairs here weren't very comfortable. He got the feeling they'd been designed that way—so nobody would ever fall asleep on the job. It wasn't that kind of starship. There was no decoration at all, other than painted colors to designate access panels.

Some panels were missing altogether, showing

bare conduits. That's how fast the project had been abandoned.

I wouldn't have abandoned it, Sisko thought. *Where one Borg came, others could come.*

The Borg had cost him worse than his life. They had cost him his wife. And if he lived on, he demanded a purpose to that life. To make sure that other cultures, other peoples' wives and families, weren't overwhelmed the way his had been. Starfleet had made a mistake dropping its plans for heavy defense just because the surface of a threat had been smoothed.

Now the halfheartedly tossed ball was here, in his hands. He wouldn't drop it.

There was no doubt that the ship's primary mission was armed, active, strong defense. There was nothing here devoted to anything else, and the bridge replicator offered only water, hot or cold. Dual consoles for Tactical and Weapons were manned at the moment by O'Brien and Kira, each quietly feeling their way across the unfamiliar panels.

T'Rul was fine-tuning the aft engineering station, from time to time bumping into O'Brien and uneasily moving away. A couple other workers and officers puttered around, making last-minute checks. Julian Bashir entered from the turbolift, nodded and smiled at Sisko, then enjoyed a long look around.

Sisko felt comfortable other than for T'Rul, the only stranger, and not exactly a passive stranger. He wanted to be left alone, but felt better than he expected to when Bashir dropped to his side on the command deck.

"The medical database is practically nonexistent," the doctor told him. "I'm downloading as many of my files from the station as I can, but this ship simply wasn't designed to handle many casualties."

They both knew what that meant—the ship wasn't meant to deal with the survival of its own crew. It expected them either to live or die. Nothing in the middle.

"Do the best you can," Sisko told him. "And let's hope your new database won't be put to the test."

Bashir didn't seem encouraged, but offered a stout nod and left Sisko alone before either was driven to say anything more in that same tone of voice.

On the upper deck, Dax entered from the corridor through the rather cranky door.

"Quark is settling into his quarters," she reported. "He asked me to relay his 'profound disappointment in the accommodations aboard this vessel' and to inform you that he could put you in touch with several reputable interior decorators for a very modest fee."

Mustering a grin for Bashir's sake, because he knew the doctor was trying to ease the moment, Sisko tried not to sound blunt. "I'll take his offer under advisement." He raised his voice to everyone. "Stand by to get under way."

The tenor of the bridge changed—subtly, but it did change.

O'Brien twisted around without taking his hands off the console he was tuning up. "Tactical and Communications ready."

"Navigation and Operations ready, sir," Dax said.

"Weapons ready," Kira sharply added.

"Impulse engines on-line," the Romulan woman said from aft. "Warp power available at your command."

Sisko nodded. "Very well," he said. "Seal the airlock. Release docking clamps. Aft thrusters at—"

"Just a moment, sir!" O'Brien called. "There's someone at the airlock."

"Visual," Sisko ordered, angry that something had shattered the near-perfect exit he'd been planning and hoping for. He wanted everything to go just right. He wanted people to talk for days, maybe months, about the beautiful and flawless launch of the daring *Defiant* and how the ship ventured through the wormhole, testimonial to the Federation's honor.

Already something had fouled.

The main monitor swarmed to life, a little sluggishly.

There was Odo, standing outside the airlock, carrying the bucket he used as a resting place when he wasn't in—well, any form at all. It looked pitiful, him standing there with his sad idea of luggage, and Sisko's anger evaporated.

"Odo . . . is there a problem?"

Uneasily, standing within embarrassing proximity to the two Starfleet guards Commander Eddington had placed at the airlock, Odo plunged in with, "No, Commander. I would like permission to come aboard." He paused, then said, "I'm here at the request of the Bajoran government."

Touched and pleased, Sisko looked up at Kira warmly. "Permission granted. And welcome aboard."

"Thank you, sir."

The screen dissolved, and Sisko anticipated the next hours, during which Odo would have to live on an unfamiliar ship, broaching the gazes of almost everybody he worked with and a few he didn't.

Sisko tipped his head toward the helm. "Dax, can you arrange quarters for the constable?"

"I'll do it, sir." Typically, Julian Bashir charged forward to mend the moment, burying the difficulty of that duty in a merry tone. "I need to go down to what is laughingly called sickbay. We're a little tight on space, sir, but I'm sure I can find something."

"Thank you, Doctor."

"Odo's on board, sir," O'Brien said. "The airlock's been cleared."

Sisko nodded at Dax. "Release docking clamps. Aft thrusters one quarter. Port and starboard at station keeping."

"Aye, sir."

The little ox of a starship hummed to life, braced for speed, and pulled away from the station docking pylon with its chin butted out and its sturdy shoulders leaning into the yoke.

Sisko couldn't help having a sad affection for the ship. Built for a purpose, then abandoned before it had a chance to do its part. Maybe he was empathizing too much with a hunk of tempered metal, but he understood too well what it was like to lose direction in life and have to stumble for a while. Could it be that the two of them had found direction together?

He had begged, harassed, demanded that Starfleet send ships of the line to come out here and defend his station, the wormhole, and that planet of refugees as they put their lives back together after throwing off the Cardassian grip. He'd pounded every desk and door from San Francisco to deep space, insisting that they couldn't afford to have a power vacuum here.

Nothing. They'd adopted too much of a no-blow-until-blows-are-struck attitude. They'd forgotten that attitudes themselves could be punitive. Combustion could go on below the surface. When the explosion came, it could be too late.

That's what had happened with the Borg. The Federation had stared like a deer in a bright light for far too long. His wife's life and thousands of others had been the price.

He shook his head, thinking inwardly of what a terrible person he was. That idea of thousands of lives—many of whom he had known . . . he hadn't been able to digest that back then. His mind had been on the few lives in his immediate perimeter. He had left Jennifer lying there dead. Other lives were at stake. His son, the people aboard the escape craft who were holding their launch for him . . . his own.

Since then, even raising his son had been bittersweet. Taking command of *Deep Space Nine*—he'd almost had to be forced to do it. He didn't want to go anywhere, do anything. Suddenly he'd found himself proprietor of a really big hotel and its lobby.

When had the turning point come? When had been the moment when he realized he had another million lives on his hands? Command of a critical point in space, control of a bridge to forever, and attendant of a section of the galaxy.

Not exactly a hotel.

And whether the Federation liked it or not, they were going to pay attention to what he thought was best out here.

He moved his hands on the arms of the command chair, felt the staunch fighting ship under him.

There had been other *Defiant*s in history, just as there were long lines of *Enterprise*s and *Hood*s and *Constitution*s. There had been other power-packed ships—the frigates of a hundred years ago, when the Klingons were a blooming threat and the Romulans a sorcery in the darkness.

Now this one stout, unfinished ship would go out under his hand and be stalwart as best it could.

He'd never commanded a ship before. This ship had never been under command before. So it was just the two of them, finding things out together.

At the helm, Dax turned to look at him for no

reason. Was he being too silent, too long? Or was she just sensing what he was thinking? Some people could do that.

She was scolding him with those flameproof eyes. She knew he was preoccupied.

Almost immediately she had to turn back to the helm to complete leaving station perimeters, but Sisko knew she'd seen the unsureness in his face. Oh, well, if his oldest friends couldn't be let in on his feelings, who could be?

"We've cleared the station," Dax said, keeping her tone level, even though it had a tinge of "wake up" in it.

"Lay in a course to the wormhole," Sisko said, letting her know with his inflections that he got the message and she was right. He turned to T'Rul and said, "I want to cloak as soon as we reach the Gamma Quadrant."

The Romulan woman had more expression in her face than he was used to from somebody who looked so much like a Vulcan. "Understood" was all she said.

"Course laid in, sir," Dax informed.

Sisko turned forward again. "Engage."

The *Defiant* sailed placidly toward the clear plot in space where the wormhole was hiding—and as the ship approached, the wormhole sensed it and bloomed to life, a great twisting golden vortex of energy, constantly beckoning, *Come to me and see if you live.*

That was always the excitement, Sisko realized as his gut tightened. Every time he sent somebody through that thing, he suppressed the underlying awe of it. Why had its inhabitants chosen to make this wormhole stable? Would they change their minds in a few years? Would some ship be going through it when someday they decided to shut it down? Nature wasn't this cooperative. Tornadoes and cyclones and wormholes weren't meant to be "stable." Every time they went through the wormhole they were making a bet that they'd make it through, then another bet that it wouldn't take sixty-seven years to get home again.

Energy crackled and spun on the main screen as though they were going down a gigantic throat. A few minutes later, and they flew out into open space—impossibly far from DS9 or Federation territory. The miracle of the wormhole made the miracle of warp speed negligible.

A wave of dizziness made Sisko realize he was holding his breath. He forced himself to inhale deeply and the dizziness went away, but left his chest aching.

He parted his lips to give an order, but never got to it. The bridge lighting dropped away. Everything white or yellow disappeared. A curtain of eerie bloodred washed over every panel, every face, giving the bridge a mood of the submarine.

"The cloaking device is operating within normal parameters," T'Rul reported.

Sisko glanced around. So this was what a cloaked ship looked like from the inside. "Set course for the Karemma system, warp seven. Engage."

At her console near O'Brien, Kira felt the first real surge of enthusiasm she'd felt in months. A real weapon, finally—a real signal that Starfleet would stick its neck out and strike in favor of the Bajorans they had promised to protect and assist.

The Bajorans needed all the help they could get, but they needed powerful help. So far, since throwing off the Cardassian oppression, they'd been collecting enemies faster than they'd been gathering friends. Starfleet regarded them as an afterthought, trying a little too hard to "respect" their sovereignty and independence, and along with Starfleet came the allied Klingons, the greedy Ferengi, the dubious Romulans . . . and now, on the other side of the wormhole, which was traversed like a street crossing by Starfleet's shuttles and runabouts—the Jem'Hadar. And the whole Dominion—and now maybe these "Founders," too.

"Triple-redundant interlocking phaser arrays," she murmured to the engineer, "multiphasic shield generators . . . quantum torpedoes . . . there's a lot of firepower crammed into this little bucket."

"Too much, if you ask me," O'Brien murmured back.

"It's my experience that there's no such thing as too much firepower, Chief."

"But all the power is reserved for the defense systems," he said. "The long-range sensors are a joke, the transporter's barely functioning, the communications system doesn't deserve the name—"

"She's fast, she's maneuverable, and she packs a hell of a punch." Kira ran her hand along the rough panel. "That's all I ask from a fighting ship."

O'Brien shrugged. "I think I prefer a little more flexibility in my ships, that's all."

"Like the *Odyssey?*" she reminded. "That was a Galaxy-class starship, Chief. One of the most versatile ships ever built. And the Jem'Hadar made short work of it. No, I'd take this ship over a more well rounded starship any day. If the Jem'Hadar want to tangle with us again, I want them to know we have teeth this time."

Quark sat on the lower bunk of a small, cramped, impolite berthing arrangement that was too tight even for him, and he wasn't very big. With the crack of the Grand Nagus's cane and Sisko's underlying ferocity still drumming in his ears, he was content to sit here alone and not wander this . . . vehicle.

They'd probably put him to work or something if he showed his face.

Over there was a tiny desk, a replicator—which didn't work. The walls were dark and depressing. The berth was claustrophobic. Probably on purpose . . . these fighting types weren't concerned about crew comforts. The whole idea was for the crew to want to get out of their quarters and stand their posts.

No problem there. Who'd want to sit in here without a good reason?

Voices—someone was coming! Kira? Was she coming to give him some kind of work to do?

Scrubbing the decks, probably. He didn't have any technical knowledge, not on a ship like this. Galley duty. If the replicators didn't work—

"Is this the best you can do?" a muffled voice asked. Not Kira.

"I'm afraid so, Constable. Space is—"

"I'll thank you not to use that term when addressing me anymore, Doctor. It no longer applies."

The hastily hung door rattled, then slid open. Quark held still. Odo and Bashir were standing there, Odo holding his bucket and Bashir looking apologetic.

"Yes, well," the doctor was saying. "I'm sorry, Odo. Most of the crew quarters don't even have life support. Besides, I think we'd all feel better with someone here to watch over Quark."

Odo frowned and peered into the dim room, and inevitably saw Quark sitting there on the mistake of a bunk.

"Odo!" Quark exclaimed.

He pushed himself off the bunk and moved toward the two of them.

That was enough to make Bashir back off.

"I'll leave you two bunkmates to get comfortable," Bashir said.

As Odo glared after him, the doctor made a quick exit down the corridor.

"Am I glad to see you!" Quark said, running his words together. "I've been stuck down here in this miserable hole since I came aboard! Bunk beds, no view, and I won't even tell you what came out of that replicator when I asked for synthehol!"

He followed Odo back into the berth, where Odo put his bucket down in a corner and tried to get comfortable on the one pitiful little chair.

Quark thought about making a crack that Odo

shouldn't be so miserable—after all, he could *become* a chair if he wanted to—but that comment probably wasn't a wise idea. Scrambling for a better idea, or even a mediocre idea, Quark realized that Odo was sitting with his back turned, completely ignoring him.

"So," Quark attempted, "what's your role in this little adventure? Providing security, no doubt. . . . Well, of course you are. I mean, why else would you be here? You're here to watch over us. Protect us from the Jem'Hadar. I can tell you I feel much safer now, just knowing that you're along, because I know you can be trusted to—"

"I've held this shape," Odo burst in flatly, "for sixteen hours. I have to revert to my liquid state, but I don't want you to watch . . . and *gawk* at me."

"I completely understand!" Quark held both hands out in a complacent offer. "This is a very private moment, and I won't interfere." He turned around, doing everything he could in these tight quarters to avoid moving his head. He didn't really believe that Odo was stripped of his rank or fired or quit or whatever had gone on back home, but pampering Odo at a bad time certainly couldn't do any harm. And something told him that there wasn't yet an end to Odo's influence over the bar and every little transaction within it.

"This won't be so bad," he went on, careful not to turn. "Sharing quarters, that is. We might even find that we—"

"I have no interest in speaking to you, or in

listening to your witless prattle. So shut your mouth and stay out of my way, or you'll regret the day you ever met me."

Too late. Chills racked Quark's spine at the gravelly words and he winced as though someone had slapped him across the face.

It was an effort to remember not to turn. Silence sank around them.

He ticked off a few long seconds, sighed a few times, ticked a few more seconds, then cautiously crawled back to his bunk.

One guarded glance at the bucket caught the last bit of Odo in his mercury-like liquid state slurping over the rim.

What else could go wrong?

"Commander, long-range scanners are picking up two Jem'Hadar warships directly ahead."

O'Brien was keeping control of his voice, but a quiver of excitement came through the steady report.

Sisko looked up, first at the engineer and then at the forward screens.

The engineer was still peering into his readouts. "They're heading this way at . . . warp five."

"How close will they pass us?"

"Three hundred thousand kilometers."

Kira turned, and she wasn't making any pretenses about whether she was excited or not. "That's well within range of their weapons, Commander."

Dax fingered the helm control. "Should I alter course?"

Sisko knew what she was thinking, what they were all thinking. Should they pounce before they were pounced upon? Make a show of power as well as stealth?

"No," he decided. "We need to know if they can see through the cloaking device and this is as good a time as any. Maintain course and speed. Red Alert."

He glanced at Kira, then looked forward again at the jewel-studded velvet of space before them, no longer empty.

"Stand by weapons and shields. . . ."

CHAPTER
5

JEM'HADAR. The new swearword. Aliens who had declared themselves enemies of the Federation they had barely met, enjoyed being so, fired without being fired upon, shot to kill at first sight, and had no intention of changing their minds.

Might as well try to negotiate with a cobra. Sisko drew a measured breath.

"Here they come. They'll pass in five seconds," O'Brien said quietly, also measuring.

"Onscreen."

The ships moved toward them, drifting in an illusion of passive slowness that was in reality high speed, in some kind of formation that changed every few seconds.

Sisko didn't bother to analyze the ships' relation to each other. He didn't care.

If the Jem'Hadar knew about cloaking devices,

or understood lateral lines held by what appeared to be natural anomalies—then it was all over. The fight would happen here and now.

If the cloak was working, that was its own kind of mandate. If the Jem'Hadar couldn't detect them under cloak, then the message was a simple one—how could the Dominion fight an invisible foe? A starship could disappear in the middle of a pursuit, or waltz through the enemy lines right up to their back door and demand negotiations.

Puffed up with possibilities, Sisko gripped the command chair and willed the cloak to work. He looked at T'Rul. She was fixed on her instruments, not moving a muscle, appearing against the syrupy Red Alert haze more like a painting of a Romulan than a living one, an image caught in the mind of one of those artists who paint exciting scenes of key points in history.

What was she thinking? Was she aware that the Romulans and the Jem'Hadar together, with the cloaking device in their hands, might defeat the Federation? If this succeeded, T'Rul would know that Romulan stock would go up in the galaxy. And the Romulans knew the Federation would never band with them to conquer anybody.

Oh, hell, where did that line of thought come from?

He gripped the chair tighter and banished the creeping suspicion.

Worry later. Succeed now.

The bridge throbbed with the heartbeats of all present. No one moved, not a flinch.

"Are they altering course?" Sisko cracked the silence.

"No, sir," O'Brien said. "They're continuing on their way. I don't think they saw us."

The relief in the chief's voice was restrained, but it was there.

Sisko let out his own breath, partly for himself and partly as a signal for his crew to start their own respiratory systems going again. If he was stupid enough to relax with Jem'Hadar ships just over his shoulder, then they might as well be too.

"Track them."

"They're continuing along their original heading," O'Brien said, complying. "No indication that they saw us or . . . Wait a minute! Heading back this way—"

"They must've seen us," Dax said.

Kira read off her console, "They're powering their weapon systems."

"Prepare to decloak," Sisko ordered. "Lock phasers on the lead ship and—"

"No!" T'Rul interrupted. "We may not have been detected."

Sisko turned to look at her. "Explain."

"A cloaked ship radiates a slight subspace variance at warp speeds—"

"A subspace variance?" O'Brien gawked at her as if she'd grown a second set of pointed ears. "I've never heard of it."

"It's not something we've been eager to reveal," the Romulan woman inflected back to him on a platter. She looked at Sisko, as though determined not to hand O'Brien any bones. "I suggest dropping out of warp. That will eliminate the variance. When they reach our position, they'll find nothing."

"Do it," he snapped to Dax.

Dax worked her helm. "All stop."

The two ships swung into view. After a beat they split up and began prowling the area of space, searching for something they thought they had seen.

"They're sweeping the area with some kind of antiproton scan," O'Brien said. "And they're being very thorough about it."

Sisko watched the ships on the screen, coming nearer by the heartbeat.

"Will an antiproton scan penetrate the cloak?"

No one answered him. There was only the sweat on his brow and the whistle of bridge noise.

He turned to look at T'Rul.

"I'm . . . not sure," she finally admitted.

Tension clicked up another notch.

"They're getting close," Kira murmured.

"Commander," O'Brien said, "the *Defiant*'s power signature is unusually high for a ship this size. The cloaking device might not be masking everything."

"Cut main power."

Almost instantly the bridge fell to darkness, lit only by two panels still operating and the glow of the main screen.

Feeling the Jem'Hadar ships gloss over the skin of his cheeks and forehead, Sisko stared at the screen.

One Jem'Hadar ship passed close enough to

touch, showing off its heavy structure down to the bolts on the hull plates.

In a moment there would be only the other ship in view. They were flanked by Jem'Hadar.

No—the nearest ship was stopping. It was right on top of them. They could put on survival suits and practically crawl to it.

With a vise around his waist, Sisko held his hands tight against his knees and watched that ship as it turned in space before them like a giant Christmas-tree ornament. There was barely a sliver of black open space left on their screen.

Sisko almost cracked when Kira's voice broke into the silence.

"The other one has broken off its search . . . it's coming this way . . ."

His own words roared inside Sisko's skull. "Stand by weapons and shields. . . ."

The Jem'Hadar vessel before them moved off slowly. The second ship came back into their screen, joining the first ship in some kind of formation.

Attack formation?

He could see their firing ports. A glow of warm-up . . .

Turning their aft quarters to the *Defiant,* the two ships powered up suddenly, and swam off together, back the way they had come.

A flash on the screen—

"They've gone into warp," Kira said, containing herself, "and resumed their original course."

Sisko didn't want to relax, to let out this breath he'd been holding, but he also knew his crew were taking his lead and if he didn't relax, they'd all die of asphyxiation.

"That's the first thing to go right in the Gamma Quadrant in a long time," he sighed.

Behind him, Kira said, "I hope it's not the last."

Karemma was a world of bureaucrats. Impolite bureaucrats. People to whom government meant the place where all decisions short of personal defection were made, and even those were under consideration. There was an obsession with order, to a point where there was nothing but order, no freshness, no comfort, no freedom. Wildflowers were discouraged.

They were mercantilists, but not in the sense that they went their own ways and did their best for themselves and their families. This was strictly controlled mercantilism, where the individual was nothing.

As such, everything had been reduced to its most efficient level, no matter the lack of quality.

Such was the manner of Ornithar, an official whose actual level of power had never been clear to Ben Sisko.

Sisko stood beside his command chair, feeling as though he were here to be statuesque and impressive. He wondered if he was pulling it off, whether Ornithar was falling for it.

Around the bridge, as though guarding their stations, his crew stood watching. Under a darkened shadow off to one side, Odo was making a presence, but deep in his own thoughts or observations.

Ornithar was busy scoping them out, inspecting their clothing, and hovering about them like a vulture, and touching parts of the bridge while Quark did most of the talking.

"The Grand Nagus himself has sent me as an emissary on his behalf. If you will aid us in our mission, I am authorized to decrease our price on tulaberry wine by . . . *three* percent."

Quark was waiting for a flamboyant reaction, but Ornithar ignored him completely and bent toward one of *Defiant*'s bulkhead struts.

"Looks like a polyduranium alloy blend. Interesting, but the metal has no real value." He straightened up and turned to Quark. "A three-percent cost reduction is negligible."

Sisko held back a sneer. No value, unless it was packed together with a whole lot of other metals and some mighty big phaser banks. No value, give or take a few people with the courage to use it.

"I have considerable leeway to bargain in this circumstance," Quark insisted. "Name your terms."

For an irrational flash, Sisko got the feeling he was being sold, lock, stock, and comm badge.

But by now Ornithar was moving on to Dax and analyzing her helm controls.

Buttons and whistles. Negotiations might be in the offing for a relationship between galactic quadrants, and this freak was looking at panel faces.

"Nothing . . . nothing . . . nothing," Ornithar grumbled. "The terms are not the issue. I cannot help you locate the Founders, because I do not know who they are. Or if they even exist."

He bent over Kira, who had the presence of being to hold still while this creature waved around beside her and considered her control panels before noticing her earring. "Here's something interesting. Appears to be diamide-laced beritium. I'll give you fifty-two diracks for it."

"Done!" Quark glanced at Sisko, and sooner than instantly got the message that he was off course. "I mean—one deal at a time, Ornithar. We're talking about the Founders."

Deprived of what he wanted, Ornithar folded his hands in front of him.

"There is nothing further to say. If the Founders exist, they clearly do not wish to be contacted. That is good enough for me."

Sisko was half a thought from snatching this crackpot by the collar and doing a little extra cracking.

"Who's your contact in the Dominion regarding administration?" he asked. "Trade? Defense?"

"Our only contact with the Dominion has been through the Vorta. I have no idea who they report to. All I know is that the Vorta say to do something . . . and you do it."

"Why?" Sisko persisted.

Ornithar smiled as if he were talking to a child. "Because if you do not, they will send in the Jem'Hadar. And then you die."

Brutal. The flatness of Ornithar's statement made Sisko think again about being lost to a repressive government. Everything the Federation's many worlds had worked for could be gone in very little time.

Beside him, Kira tightened up too. He noticed her hands turn white and ball into fists. Her thoughts were probably less philosophical than his. After all, she'd lived through what he feared most, what most humans regarded as history.

The message was clear enough and blunt enough, but somehow still held the vague non-answers clinging to this quadrant and its hostile denizens. No one wanted to say anything precise. Everything was a warning carved on a rock. No clues of who had cut it there.

"Can you describe the Vorta?" Dax began, changing the tack of questioning.

Sisko found his intestines settling a little at the sound of her rational question. She must have sensed that he was about to gut-punch an answer out of this maggot.

Ornithar pondered the question—which was idiotic, since he obviously knew what he was going to say. "Physically," he said eventually, "they're humanoid . . . with limited telekinetic abilities."

"Telekinetic," Dax repeated with unmasked surprise.

Sisko looked at her and she looked back, and they both knew the conclusion.

Sisko couldn't tell if this galactic flea-market dealer was guarding his reaction or if he was really annoyed by a possible customer's knowing what he was thinking.

He felt his eyes burn with intensity. "Will you put us in contact with the Vorta? They may help us locate the Founders."

"Commander," Ornithar said, laden with passive disinterest, "we do what we're told, nothing more. And so far, we have not been told to help you in any way."

"But you have not been told to hinder us either."

"No, but I prefer to err on the side of caution."

Quark came to life again—did he see a way in?

"In this case," he interrupted, "being cautious will cost you the Ferengi trade in tulaberry wine. The Nagus will stop all shipments immediately."

Sisko almost shrugged and shook his head with frustration that Quark—that anybody—would think such a threat carried any weight in galactic matters, but the maggot actually looked concerned.

So Sisko pushed. "If you lost such a valuable contract, it might displease the Vorta. They might even send the Jem'Hadar here to find out what happened."

To his complete amazement, the turkey across the bridge twitched a couple times and started to gobble.

"I will need to access one of our computers on the surface."

After Sisko motioned him toward a panel, Ornithar went to it, worked it briefly—with little effort too. Evidently this chicken was brighter than he let on, to be able to work alien controls after a cursory study.

A star chart flooded into place on the main viewer.

"This is the Callinon system," Ornithar said. "The Dominion maintains an unmanned subspace relay station on the seventh planet. We have been told by the Vorta to direct all communications there. Where the messages are sent after that is not our concern."

Wondering if this wasn't all a little too simple, Sisko looked at Dax.

"It's a start," she said. She seemed pleased, and that was a good change.

"But what you do from that point is your affair," Ornithar hastily pointed out. "And remember—all I've done is point you in a direction! I've told you nothing else!"

"We understand," Sisko told him, just barely managing to keep the patronization out of his voice.

Ornithar looked at each of them as if they were about to hold up score signs on his performance and he'd forgotten to bribe the judges.

Nobody held up any cards, but just held still and waited for him to do what he was just committed to do, good or bad.

"What is *that?*"

Odo's sudden ejection into movement startled everybody. Sisko barely managed to stifle a flinch —he'd almost forgotten Odo was back there.

They all turned to see him pointing at a symbol on the opposite side of the star map from where Ornithar was indicating.

Ornithar blinked in confusion, then said, "It is the Omarion Nebula."

Odo seemed transfixed by the symbol—more. Captured. Drawn.

He moved toward the screen.

"The Omarion Nebula," he croaked, tasting the sounds.

His eyes fell away from the star map and he turned from the rest of them, going back into his own thoughts. With him he took the branded-in memory of that star map.

Sisko could see the weight of this new thing straining Odo as the shapeshifter wandered to the far side of the bridge and remained turned away from them.

"If there's nothing else," Ornithar suffered, "I would like to leave now."

"Of course." Sisko grabbed at the opportunity to get his crew to stop gaping at poor Odo.

As he herded them toward the door, Quark pulled his arm. "Commander, I believe I have fulfilled my role on this mission, so if you don't mind—"

"You'd like to stay behind."

"That *was* our agreement. . . ."

Sisko glanced at Ornithar, then angled Quark aside. "How can you be sure he won't turn you over to the Dominion as soon as we leave?"

Quark got a hurt expression, trying to imply that he was an expert judge of character. "He may serve the Dominion, but I'm the one lining his pockets with latinum. I'll get passage on the next freighter back through the wormhole. And I'll make a profit in the process."

Encouraged by their one bit of luck and clinging to it with both hands, Sisko couldn't help a brief smile at Quark's relentlessness. One thing he had to give the Ferengi, however much a pest, however much a leech: Quark had a sense of what he wanted in life and his grip on that purpose seldom wavered.

Not everybody had that, never mind the approval of others.

And Quark had done his job, despite his obvious fear and unwillingness to come here at all. Sisko couldn't help admiring him for that.

When he looked into Quark's expressive, if somewhat clownish, eyes right now, he didn't see an annoyance or a pest. He saw another man, of surprising intelligence, who had a different row to plow than his own.

With this part over, Quark would no longer be in the sphere of immediate danger. Sisko would no longer be forcing an unwilling participant into the boiling pot.

"All right," he offered warmly. "Good luck, Quark."

"Same to you, Commander."

As Ornithar exited without a glance, Sisko turned to Dax. "Lay in a course for the Callinon system."

He took her acknowledging glance without reaction, and as he turned back to the forward screen, Quark was still beside him, now leaning closer. "There is one other thing . . . something is very wrong with Odo."

Sisko nodded. "I'm aware of his frustration about being relieved—"

"It's more than that. He's . . . different somehow. I've known him a long time and I've never seen him like this before." He grew quieter still, and leaned still closer. "I know this sounds strange . . . but I'm worried about him."

Suddenly wondering how many bizarre altera-
tions he was going to have to deal with in his usual
measurement of those around him, Sisko regarded
Quark with still more simmering respect.

"I'll try to keep an eye on him," he promised.

Quark seemed satisfied for now, and left with the
others. Sisko felt the extra measure of responsibility shift onto him with that promise, not only to
watch over their lives, but their spirits as well.

Even Odo, who always had been so solitary—but
not solitary enough to keep from eliciting devotion
from an unlikely source.

Validating his expanded duty, he paused at the
threshold. "Odo?"

For a moment he thought he might have to call
again.

Then Odo broke from his reverie and came
toward him, passed him, and went out, without
ever once meeting his eyes.

Sisko tried to relax in his quarters, and in fact
found it easier to do in these bare bunks than he
had for the first three months in his homelike
quarters on the station. Somehow this soldier-bare
pup-tent living was comforting. Probably because
it reminded him of a time when he wasn't the one
making any decisions. When he was quartered in
bunks like these, there had always been a commander or a captain to do the worrying.

Of course, he had always participated in the
usual rumors and second-guessing, but the commanders had all the fretting and deciding to do.

Ah, those were the days. Deckhand days. Every deckhand dreams of being a captain. Every captain dreams of being a deckhand.

Oh, well . . .

The fog began to close in and he was almost asleep. Almost—the door chime blasted like an alert klaxon.

He forced himself up and swung his legs off the bed.

"Come in."

It was Kira. "Did I wake you?"

"Not quite," he said. "What can I do for you, Major?"

She started pacing. Or maybe she just had that set about her, because there wasn't anywhere in here to pace to.

"It's about Odo. . . ."

He peered at her in the dimness. The lights weren't very good, and at the moment he was glad.

"You're worried about him," he supposed.

She paused. "Is it that obvious?"

"No. It's just that everyone seems worried about Odo right now. So am I, for that matter. But at the moment, I'm not sure what to do about it."

Kira came into the room and sat down in the excuse for a chair. "May I speak freely?"

He was careful to nod, only that and only once. Kira could go off like a firecracker, but almost always flaring in a direction he couldn't ignore.

"What the hell is wrong with Starfleet?" she chafed. "How could they do this to him?"

"This has been a long time coming. Starfleet has *never* been happy with the constable. They've been quietly but firmly pressing me to replace him for two years."

Her bright eyes blazed in the dimness. "Because he used to work for the Cardassians."

"No," he cut off quickly. "It goes deeper than that. In their view . . . he's not a 'team player.'"

"Well, neither was I!—at first."

"They weren't too crazy about you either, Major. But you've changed . . . lost that chip on your shoulder and stopped suspecting us all of trying to subvert Bajor." He offered a tempering smile. "I could probably even get you a Starfleet commission at this point."

"Let's not go too far." She might have been smiling, but in the bad light he couldn't tell.

If she wasn't, he didn't want to know.

"You know Odo," he said. "He enjoys thumbing his nose at authority. He files reports only when *he* feels like it. His respect for the chain of command is minimal—"

"So what? He gets the job done."

"I know, but Starfleet likes team players, Major. They like the chain of command. And when you get right down to it . . . so do I."

"So you agree with their decision?"

"No. But I understand it."

"So when this mission's over," she concluded, "you're just going to let him leave?"

"I want him to stay as much as you do," he told her. "But he has to *want* to stay."

Kira thought about that for a long time. Sisko could almost hear her mind clicking, adding up what they all knew about Odo, and how much they didn't, all the times he had demanded more of himself than he would ever have asked of anyone else.

"I've known him for a long time," she said, "and I have to tell you, with all due respect . . . I think you're wrong. I think what's really bothering him now isn't the loss of his position or that his pride has been wounded. I don't think he wants to leave *us*. He doesn't have a family, he doesn't have other friends, he doesn't even know where he came from." She was forward almost far enough for her elbows to rest on her knees, her body tense and knotted with emotion, her eyes shining the way they did when she believed something enough to push the issue. Her fingers spread across the front of her uniform, barely touching the fabric. "We're all he has," she surged. "He *is* a team player, Commander. He just doesn't go by the same rules."

Frustration galled her features when the comm rang and T'Rul's voice interrupted them.

"Bridge to Commander Sisko. We've reached the Callinon system."

Sisko apologized to Kira with his glance, but it wasn't good enough. He felt as though he was somehow letting down not just her, but Odo too, because right now he had to shunt both of them aside because something else was up.

How could he say that to her?

He got up and gestured her toward the door. "On my way."

"Ship's log, stardate 48213.1. We have arrived at Callinon VII under cloak and assumed a standard orbit. The relay station on this planet should not only help us in our search for the Founders, but should also provide us a first glimpse at the technology of the Dominion."

Atmospheric gases swirled in patterns almost purposeful, carrying clouds and storms along large oceans. In fact, everything about this planet was large, muscular, massive. Yet its forests and mountain ranges recalled Earth, and Ben Sisko suddenly wished he'd stalled his "vacation" just a week or two longer.

Even though it had been good to get back to DS9, he still wanted Jake to have a memory of Earth. His emotions ricocheted again. That sense of place, of past—he was thinking of Odo.

He squeezed out those thoughts and concentrated on the planet below.

A graphic of the Callinon relay station flickered on one of the monitors while he and the whole bridge crew waited for Kira's report.

"From our sensor sweeps," she finally said, "it looks like Ornithar was telling the truth when he claimed the relay station was unmanned. There also appear to be very few security measures in place."

Sisko took that as good enough. He turned to Dax and O'Brien, who stood on the aft bridge, armed and equipped with phasers and tricorders.

"Nothing fancy," he told them. "Get in, find out what we need, and get out."

"Understood," Dax said.

"On your way."

As they hurried out the bridge exit, he spun to T'Rul.

"The transporter will need three seconds to beam them down. I want to decloak for *exactly* three seconds."

With just enough reaction to remind him she wasn't Vulcan, she nodded and put her hand on her controls. He couldn't tell from that whether or not she was sure she could do it, or she was determined to try.

Either way, nothing he could say could change her abilities. If the Romulan Empire thought Starfleet needed a baby-sitter for their trickery, then let her baby-sit. The mechanics of being cloaked were her problem.

He had others.

"Dax to bridge. We're ready, Benjamin."

"All right. T'Rul, disengage cloak." He turned to Kira. "Energize."

T'Rul worked her instruments furiously as Kira worked her own. The bridge lights flushed, then came up as the cloak was turned off.

"They're on the surface," Kira said.

Sisko glanced at T'Rul, but she was already working. Again darkness flooded around them as the cloak was brought back on-line.

Clear relief shone on the Romulan woman's face.

There was something about that change in her that bothered him. Yes, Romulans were hostile and emotional, but dangerously similar to their fore-bears in appearance and manner. That severe dark, glossy hair cut like a helmet, those demonic eyes and angled ears. They could be stoic, mysterious, hedge every question . . . and their greatest advantage was that they were so like Vulcans on the surface that people of the Federation could be tempted to take them at their word.

Sisko determined not to. Not quite yet, anyway.

"Were we scanned during transport?" he asked.

"I don't think so," Kira said. "It looks like the array is strictly an automated relay station. Very few security measures."

"All the same, keep a transporter lock on Dax and O'Brien in case we have to pull them out of there fast."

Kira glanced at him. Sisko realized he'd just given away his tension by telling her what he had just told Dax.

"Aye, sir" was all she said.

"Dax to *Defiant.*"

"Go ahead, Dax," he said.

"We're in what seems to be the central computer room. The user interface is a little unusual, but I think we can access it."

"Keep us posted."

In the background down there, O'Brien said, "I'm into the main directory."

"That was fast," Dax said.

"Yes, it was. A little too fast, if you ask me."

"Any sign that we've tripped some kind of security protocol?" Dax rightly inquired.

Sisko almost interrupted, but held back. In a few seconds, O'Brien's voice filtered through the open line. "No. I still have access to everything."

"Then let's get the information and get out of here."

"Fine with me."

The team fell to silence, and here on the bridge, everyone else sat on the edge of their work.

Bashir appeared at Sisko's side with a cup of coffee, a tiny pool of civilization in the unending mist. A cup of history, every bit as much part of human heritage as those artifacts Sisko and Jake had unpacked.

Ah, coffee. The triumphant bean. From Constantinople to Camus II, from Paris to New Paris Colony, coffeehouses had bred poems and plots, service and subterfuge. The Earthborn substance was still more popular in the settled galaxy than anything else Quark could wrangle. Women had petitioned against it, races had forbidden it, political strife had been provoked by it, corruption had followed it, and games had been invented to play around it.

And here he was, carrying it seventy thousand miles. He found himself thinking back on all the myriad items and customs and even diseases that had come across oceans and space on ships like this, so common that nobody gave them a second look when there was a bigger goal at stake.

At the Federation's Thomas Jefferson Memorial Rose Garden, somebody had shown him a yellow and pink rose whose ancestry could be traced back to a packet of seeds smuggled out of France on the last transport before Nazi occupation.

And he was pretty sure that under those conditions, nobody was thinking about the seeds.

The flower was called "Peace."

Maybe I should've brought the rose instead of coffee.

Sisko gazed down into the steaming cup. With just one dot of kahlua . . .

Oh, well—here's to small things.

He pressed his lip to the brim of the cup and took a sip, and almost threw up.

His lips curdled as he looked around for a place to spit this out.

How would that look? So he swallowed it and was thrust into the lovely land of aftertaste.

"I should've taken Quark up on his offer for a new replicator. . . ."

Bashir looked around at him again. "Sir?"

"Nothing."

He handed the cup of future back to Bashir and moved to the command area near Kira.

"Let's make good use of this time, Major," he said. "Begin running a level-three diagnostic on—"

"Dax to *Defiant*. I think we have something, Benjamin. We've found a communications log of recent outgoing transmissions."

Before any response could be made, O'Brien added, "From the way I read this, sir, it looks like eighty percent of the outgoing traffic is sent to one location. It's my guess that's either another relay station, or some kind of command center."

"Do you have the coordinates of that location?" Sisko asked.

The chirp of Dax's tricorder came over the comm lines. "I'm sending them to you now."

Kira moved to another console. "Receiving the

coordinates. Wait a minute—I've lost contact with the away team! I'm picking up some kind of power surge on the surface!"

Through the open frequencies blasted alarms that were impulsively ringing through from down on the planet.

"Get them out of there!" Sisko shouted.

"I can't." Kira worked and reworked her console. "Some kind of shield just appeared around the outpost. I can't get through it!"

New warning whistles suddenly went off at the tactical console. Bashir dived for them, and looked abruptly horrified.

"We're picking up three Jem'Hadar ships, Commander! They're heading for the outpost!"

Kira jumped to confirm, and evidently saw what Bashir did. "Dax and O'Brien must've triggered some kind of alarm."

Sisko jumped to help her with the controls. "Can we punch through that security shield with our phasers before those ships get here?"

"I'm not sure—I've never seen a field like this before."

T'Rul urgently said, "In order to use the phasers, we will have to decloak. That means we will be seen by the Jem'Hadar."

Bashir turned to Sisko. "We have to do something! We can't just leave them down there!"

"That's exactly what we should do, Doctor," T'Rul said. "Leave them. We came here to find the Founders, not to fight the Jem'Hadar over two expendable crew members."

Unusual fury erupted in Bashir's eyes. "No one is expendable."

"The Jem'Hadar ships have entered the system," Kira said. "They'll be in orbit in thirty seconds."

Everyone watched Sisko. His midsection was tight as a corset, his face stiff and his neck so knotted he wondered if he could speak at all.

"Prepare to leave orbit," he said. "Lay in a course to the coordinates Dax sent us."

He saw the way Kira and Bashir were looking at him, and deliberately didn't look back.

Finally Kira dropped to the helm and laid the course in.

"Commander," Bashir began.

"As you were, Doctor."

Kira didn't glance up. "Course laid in."

"Warp seven," Sisko said. "Engage."

CHAPTER
6

"WE'VE LEFT the Jem'Hadar sensor range . . . there's no sign of pursuit, Commander."

There was no satisfaction in Kira's report. In fact, there was a hint of bald disappointment.

"Very well." Sisko knew Kira was hoping the Jem'Hadar would follow the ship instead of investigating the planet.

A small part of him had been hoping they would do that too, and there was mixed pleasure, ragged relief in finding out that the Jem'Hadar had failed to see the wobble of space that would give away the presence of a cloaked ship. They'd just left their crewmates behind on that planet.

He could simply turn and order T'Rul to decloak the ship, and he could turn and fight. Dax and O'Brien surely knew by now that they had been abandoned—what would Dax think?

Drop cloak, turn, and really test this ship in battle . . . he hungered for one shred of logic that would let him do that at this stage.

Two people's lives up against the millions on Bajor, the billions in the Federation—Sisko shook away the damnation he felt about leaving those two behind, and demanded of himself that this mission wouldn't start a war if he could help it.

If he could help it.

Bashir stood back there at the Ops station and simmered. "Commander, you were captured by the Jem'Hadar . . . what do you think will happen to Dax and O'Brien?"

"They'll probably be held for interrogation. If I know Dax, she'll continue with the mission and try to use this opportunity to contact the Founders. I intend to do the same." He steadied himself and tapped the comm. "Sisko to Odo. Please report to the bridge, Constable. I want to discuss the security arrangements for our arrival."

There wasn't any response for several seconds. He wondered if Odo could hear him while in that liquid state. He'd never really thought about the physics of Odo's natural condition. Did Odo need humanoid ears to hear the comm? Of course, he needed a humanoid mouth to respond—

"I'm presently . . . indisposed, Commander. Please find someone else for the job."

Sisko glanced at his officers, then took his hand off the comm and let it click off.

"That doesn't sound like Odo," Bashir observed.

"No, it doesn't," Sisko agreed. "I think I'd better have a talk with him."

Aware of the cold compassion in his voice, he suddenly didn't want to talk to Odo. He didn't want to subject himself or Odo to the critical facts—that this mission was too important for self-pity. Odo's behavior could reduce their efficiency. Odo was going to have to put away his feeling, just as Sisko was having to put away what he felt about never seeing Dax and O'Brien again, and about what they were thinking of him when they understood that he had thrown them to the wolves.

He started to get out of his command chair, but Kira was at his side now—and she was stopping him.

"Let me, sir," she offered. "I think I can talk to him."

He felt somehow that he should be doing this, not shunting it off on a volunteer, but with Jem'Hadar on his tail, a Romulan on his bridge, and two officers missing, he was glad to give her the nod and let her take one of these weights off his shoulder.

And was it significant of something else? Had he let Odo down in the past months? Shouldn't he be the one who thought he could get through?

Kira was already gone. To catch her back and take her place belowdecks would be a mistake now.

"Three Jem'Hadar ships have just entered sensor range, bearing zero three seven, mark two one five."

He turned his attention to the screen.

"Any sign they detected us?"

"Negative," T'Rul said bluntly.

"Bring us out of warp, then cut main power. We'll wait here until they pass."

As she approached the quarters that Odo had shared with Quark and now occupied alone, Kira girded herself with a dozen anecdotes and incidents that had helped her live through her difficult past. She didn't even buzz the door chime. If he was compromised, too bad.

She had to pause at the open door to adjust her eyes to the dimness. For a few moments all that showed in the darkness was the small computer monitor screen at the desk. It threw a waxy glow on Odo's face, until both it and he appeared inanimate.

His attention was fixed on the glowing screen. It showed the star chart they had all seen in Ornithar's office. Odo gazed, as if drugged, at the chart.

"Odo," Kira began, "it's time we had a talk."

"I'm not going to the bridge, so don't waste your breath. And I would appreciate being left alone right now."

"All I've done is leave you alone." She moved into the tiny quarters. "And it hasn't done any good. So maybe it's time you stopped brooding and started talking."

Stop, talk . . . she'd said that as though she had the foggiest clue what he had to talk about. She hoped he wouldn't notice she was trying to jump over the puddle of her own ignorance between them.

He turned and gave her a bitter look. "Are you the ship's counselor now?"

She came around and leaned against the bunk, looking down at him. "No. I'm your friend. You know—the person that usually comes to you when she needs help. I'm just trying to return the favor."

"You can return the favor by giving me a shuttlecraft and letting me go."

The request—blunt though it was—took her completely off guard. A shuttlecraft? Out here?

"Go?" she reacted. "Go where? We're in the heart of the Dominion. Where the hell do you think you're going to go?"

He pointed at the small screen. "The Omarion Nebula."

She frowned at it. "Why?"

"I'm not sure why. But I have to go. That's all I know."

Almost grinning, she folded her arms. "You're going to have to do a lot better than that."

He turned away from her, rejected her, whatever help or comfort she would try to give. Was he practicing for a more permanent disruption of all these relationships he had built even against his own will?

Funny how loyalties could sneak up from behind.

His voice was rough.

"Ever since we've come into this Gamma Quadrant, I've had this feeling that I'm being drawn somewhere . . . pulled by some instinct to a specific place. I think it might be . . . the Omarion Nebula."

Within the plastic mask of an unfinished human

face, Odo's clear and piercing eyes were fogged with disturbance, displaying not a passion or a hunger to go where he was bidden, but an unbidden magnetism to go there.

"Why there?" she asked.

"I don't know."

"Based on what?"

"A feeling . . . an overpowering feeling that if I go there I will find the answers to what I've been searching for all my life."

Vague, vague.

Kira's brow wrinkled. She'd come with easy talk about friendship, hoping to segue into clarity, and had ended up with an armful of troubling gray areas. What could she do? Ask him to be specific before she went to bat for him? He obviously didn't have the answers to give.

Odo had never put stock in the mystic, she knew. He barely tolerated the religion of Bajor intruding on his jurisdiction. He believed in the tangible and the noncontradictory. That was what made him good at his job.

His former job.

"All right," she said, resigned. "Once we've contacted the Founders, I'm sure Commander Sisko will—"

"No! Not after we've contacted the Founders. *Now*—I have to leave *now.*"

"Look," she bargained, "I know how much this means to you, but we have a mission to complete."

He turned to her, anger pleating his eyes and a fury in his posture that she had never seen—not this way.

She backed away from his desperation, giving room to his surging pain and letting him know she didn't mean to press him away from his needs.

The room—the whole ship—rocked sharply to one side. Kira staggered and nearly fell, her mind spinning with conclusions about what was happening—had they hit something? Had the engines shut down? What would they do about the engines without O'Brien on board?

A foot from her, Odo stumbled into the desk, his lanky arms waving for balance.

Without giving them time for a second breath, a force of wind and power blew the bulkhead in. Metal that had been part of the ship became torn scrap, and flushed across the little room as light from the corridor flooded in. Kira stole a second to turn her face upward, trying to see what was happening, but all she saw was the torn structural members of the wall coming down on top of them both.

"Direct hit on the port nacelle," T'Rul reported, raising her voice over the *boom* that tumbled through the *Defiant* under enemy fire.

Three Jem'Hadar ships had approached off the port bow. Were these the same three they had avoided only minutes ago, or was it a tactical habit that they traveled in threes?

Sisko raked his mind for answers. He'd held course when the three ships showed no sign of having detected them.

Now things were suddenly different.

"How did they see through the cloaking device?" Bashir typically blurted.

Glaring at the screen, Sisko scoured his experience for the wild answers. "Is it possible they could always see through it? They were just waiting for the right moment?"

The doctor gaped at him. "You mean it's a trap?"

Sisko turned a steamy glance on T'Rul, and got what he expected. It *was* possible that the Jem'Hadar were laughing at their cloak, thinking of the *Defiant* as a child who covers his own eyes and says, "You can't see me."

Suddenly the Romulan woman looked anything but arrogant. That meant he might be right.

"They might have analyzed the sensor information," she said, "from their antiproton scan and found a way to penetrate the cloak."

Grimly Sisko regained attention and reminded them to concentrate by saying, "We'll have to save speculation for later. Disengage cloak, raise shields, and prepare to fire on my command."

Lighting on the bridge changed as power was rerouted and the power-packed starship showed herself in the wide arena of space.

Unfaltering, the *U.S.S. Defiant* got her first chance to spread her claws and do what she was designed to do. She sighted down her enemies, and prepared to face three evil-eyed cockerels of the Jem'Hadar.

"T'Rul, take engineering," Sisko ordered, turning to each of them. "Doctor, you're at the helm. I'll handle tactical—"

The ship careened to starboard as a glancing blow rammed along her side.

"Minor hit on deck three," T'Rul said. "Communications and long-range sensors are out."

Didn't need either of those—Sisko worked his console as if he had three hands. "I'm locking the lead ship into the fire-control system."

Facing the main screen, Sisko fixed his glare on the two ships he could still see maneuvering on their perimeter.

"Fire."

"I've lost contact."

"So have I. Can you pick up anything on your tricorder?"

"From space? Thanks for the compliment, Lieutenant, but no."

"You're welcome. But I meant locally. Any changes?"

"No, and I sure am trying. I'd like to get these damned alarms to cut off. Let me try the other side of the room . . . never heard so much clatter—"

"These monitors are dead."

"What'd you say?"

"I said the monitors are dead."

"They've got some kind of automatic shutdown. I'm trying to trace it. Looks like it's over there. . . ."

"I think . . . should . . . alone."

"What?"

"I *think* . . . leave it alone!"

Miles O'Brien looked back across the expanse of the technical outpost they had discovered and had been peacefully investigating when everything had started to go wrong. Until ten seconds ago he'd been over there beside her, looking at the monitors as they flashed coded information at them. Now he was across this large, low-ceilinged deck area, halfway under a console, their voices drummed out by an inharmonic wail of klaxons and warning whistles that made Red Alert on a starship sound like a church bell choir.

He stopped what he was trying to do when Dax waved at him. Why did she want him to stop? He straightened, came back toward her, and glanced around the room, frustrated now that he couldn't try to make the noise stop.

"What've you got in mind?" he asked as he joined her.

"If we did something to set these off," she said, "then we're already in trouble. If not, then we'd better not be the ones to—"

The bells fell off, and a thought later, the klaxons. Echoes pealed through their heads, then also drowned in quiet.

Dax sighed. "Oh, I don't like this. . . ."

Beside her, O'Brien shook the pounding out of his skull. "Did you send a complete set of coordinates back to the *Defiant* about the location of the signal traffic?"

"I don't know. I hope so," she told him, "because I think they've been forced to veer off. Otherwise they'd be beaming us off. Since they're not, I have to assume they were forced to cloak."

He felt a pallor wash through his ruddy cheeks. "You think they left us?"

"Or they're trying to create a diversion."

"I know what you're saying." He nodded in tense agreement with himself. "The mission is more important than we are."

"We've got to batten down here," she said. "Give them a chance to come back for us."

Taking pause from panic just for a moment, O'Brien watched the lithe dark-haired woman as she strode the room for possibilities. Jadzia Dax remained a kind of mystery to him, like a story that haunted him but whose message lay under the surface.

Like Irish poetry, he noted. That old stuff that his Mum tried to make him appreciate.

What could have made her peaceful with a mind . . . That nobleness made simple as a fire . . . With beauty like a tightened bow, a kind that is not natural in an age like this . . . being high and solitary and most stern? Why, what could she have done being what she is? . . . Was there another Troy for her to burn?

He'd never had a clue what any of that should mean, because he turned almost as dead an ear to the history as he had to the poetry. But he thought of it as he watched Dax's profile while she touched a console. He remembered his mother's voice and the roll of her eyes as she tried to communicate the significance that flew right over this boy's noggin. She had wanted him to be *so* Irish. And he'd wanted to make lights go on in the dark and machines work that were broken.

Oh, well. Poetry wasn't for everybody.

Except Jadzia. She was a poem, one of those strange ones with a secret.

Kind of like that worm living inside her, where all the brains were.

Imagine having a worm inside, hitching a ride for life, with three hundred years of experiences all stored up. He couldn't fathom it. There'd been every manner of alien coming and going through his tenure with Starfleet and he could get along with the strangest of them, but there was something so parasitic about the Trills, the whole manner of having some animal inside . . . if a man fell in love with Jadzia Dax, who would he be loving?

O'Brien shook his head to beat down the willies and wanted to get home to his wife and daughter. Sometimes he just needed the basics. Man, woman, lots of babies. And maybe he'd give his parents a call.

A wall-mounted console burped and whistled off to his side. He ran over there and tried to make sense of the unfamiliar markings.

"I think forcefields just came up," he said. "God knows where, though."

"To protect us or keep us in?" Dax came back toward him.

"No idea. Uh-oh . . . there goes the systemwide readout. Ships coming in!"

He looked at her.

"How many?" she asked, unflapped as ever.

"Doesn't say."

"We've got to get out of here."

O'Brien turned to her. "And go where? This

place is a rock. We've got no survival gear—I'm not even sure about the atmosphere."

"No, we have to stay in this complex. There's no animal life. They'd pick the two of us up on sensors almost immediately in an open area. How big is this terminal?"

"Judging from information I picked up on the *Defiant,* it's about two square kilometers—Damn! Somebody's beaming down!" He pointed at the jumping sensors on his own tricorder.

Quickly Dax gathered her tricorder and other handhelds. "How are you at stealth?"

With a buried shudder O'Brien scooped up his own equipment. "I've got some survival ideas. Let's give 'em a whirl."

They ran for the nearest exit as the whine of transporter energy filled the area behind them.

"I hear transporters," he said. "Must be a couple dozen."

"You can tell from the sound?"

"I can *guess* from it," he admitted.

His guess was apparently good enough for her. She moved a little faster.

She ducked before him into a narrow corridor— very narrow, wide enough for two of them or maybe one Jem'Hadar at a time. O'Brien skidded around the corner, then paused to look back.

A couple dozen Jem'Hadar soldiers now stood where a moment ago the two of them had been standing.

"Go, go," he whispered, nudging her forward. He had no idea what kind of tracking equipment those creatures possessed.

Dax led the way through dim corridors, all packed with equipment of various kinds. The mechanical stuff even lined the ceiling over their heads. Without time for analysis, O'Brien knew he wouldn't be able to tell life support from the lunch counter.

"Wait!" He stopped suddenly. Without pausing, he started turning on some of the electronics around him.

Dax was waiting for him at the next corner, phaser drawn.

When he joined her, he said, "Switch on everything you see for the first three minutes. Processors and maintenance machines, anything else we see. Then we'll veer off and hope they have trouble tracking us. It might blind their sensors—at least, that's what I'm *guessing*."

"What keeps them from turning it all off?"

"This does." He had been hoping she'd ask. Leveling his phaser at the controls, he blasted his daughter's initials into the surface mechanism. Sparks drenched them both. The mechanism melted.

Dax lit up the dim corridor with her smile. "I like the way you think."

Stiffly he nodded, but couldn't muster a smile to hand back to her, and felt bad about it ten seconds later. By then, she was already halfway down the next corridor.

"There must be a schematic of these halls," she said. "We should get out of them."

"Where'll we go?"

"A subspace relay station isn't exactly a radio on

a pad, Chief. This is a complex place. If we can get into the guts of these mechanics and follow an arbitrary path, we'll double chances that they won't be able to track us."

"I'm all for it," O'Brien responded. "But don't forget what that does to the chances of Commander Sisko finding us if he comes back here."

"Oh, I don't intend to wait for that," Dax said as she pried off a wall panel.

"Not that one," O'Brien said. "That's just surface access. Let's try this one over here. It's bigger. What is it you've got in mind?"

"We have a mission," she reminded. "We should try to follow through on it."

Astonished, he glowered at her while hammering a wall seam apart with the butt of his phaser. "That's daft. Here in the middle of a swarm of these bumblebees? They'll kill us on sight."

"Not if we see them first."

It seemed she was unremitting. He could tell she was thinking, dreaming up a plan while she helped him dismantle the wall.

"Don't bend it," he said as he lifted the dislodged panel and set it at his feet. "We have to get it back on or they'll know where we went. You know, you're talking about going on the offensive. You realize that, don't you?"

"Yes. Something you said a moment ago . . . you've given me an idea."

"I have? Here, let's have you get in here first. I'll pull up the panel."

As she arranged her long legs and torso into the

innards of the wall, he did his best to keep his eyes where they belonged.

"Hustle up, there," he said. "I can hear them coming."

"What you said about bumblebees." Her voice was muffled by the insulation in the walls. "We have to snare one of the Jem'Hadar."

O'Brien crawled in after her, then managed to crank around and retrieve the wall section. It wouldn't fit back in.

"What do you want one for? Autopsy, I hope."

Far into the machinery now, Dax sounded very faint. "No, no. Alive. Tangle him in a web long enough to talk to him."

"We could stun—" O'Brien bit his tongue as the wall panel slipped through his fingers and bumped the deck with one corner.

The corner bent as it hit. Would it fit back in now? He tried again, trying to maneuver his thick fingers to do what pinchers and magnets were meant to do.

Scrapes and voices down the corridor lanced him with panic. He fought to control himself and bring the wall section up slowly, fit it properly.

"We could stun one," he said quietly.

She didn't answer. Probably didn't want to raise her voice.

The top of the wall section went in all right this time, but he was still holding the bottom edge with two fingers. If he could just leave those two fingers behind, everything would be fine.

"Here." Dax's voice was right over his shoulder.

He drew a hard breath. "You scared me!"

"Shh. Here." In her hand was one of the things she used to keep her long hair slicked back and tied between her shoulder blades. It had a decorative piece, and a thin metal part with a small hook.

"Oh, that's good, great, just right." The metal part of the barrette fit right where his fingers had gone. There wasn't much leverage, and the barrette wasn't strong, but it held long enough for him to tug the bottom of the wall panel almost into place. "It's wedged in. I don't think—"

"Let's go, then."

The service passage was a head-bumper and the devil on their knees as they made their way deep into the relay station's guts. They took several arbitrary turns and climbed one rickety ladder that hadn't been used in years, judging by the rust all over it and the detached tines.

"We have to capture one of the Jem'Hadar," Dax thought aloud. "Long enough to talk to him."

"Uch, that gives me the worms. Sorry—nothing personal."

She looked back at him and smiled again, but didn't say anything.

"I could try to find one alone and stun him," he offered, completely unable to imagine what she was going to tell one of these monkeys to get him to do their bidding.

"We can't drag a creature that large around the station for ten minutes until it comes out of it," she said. "You've got to think more brutal than that, Chief."

He rubbed his ear after snagging it on a piece of

plastic sticking out into their pathway. "Now, look, I can be as brutal as the next man. I'd take that personally if I weren't a roaring coward."

"All right." She found a bare spot and sat down, inching around to face him, and pulled her tricorder strap until the instrument lay on her lap. "Let's see where they are."

O'Brien squatted and tried to spare his aching knees.

Her tricorder clicked faintly as it searched for life-forms below them.

"Three to our right . . . thirty meters . . . four more in that direction . . . fifty-two meters . . . one behind you . . . eighty meters . . . one behind me . . ." She dropped her volume abruptly and looked up. "Ten meters!"

O'Brien hiked up onto one knee and brought his phaser around—just in case. "That's our boy," he whispered.

Forcing herself around onto her knees, Dax ducked her head so her back-combed hair wouldn't catch in the machinery. She had a job on her hands to bundle up her long frame and limbs enough to inch through this passage. O'Brien noted that he was as tall as she was, but he somehow folded up into a package better than she could.

They followed the tricorder's directional sensor, but had to double back twice to find passages they could get through and still follow the targeted soldier as he made his way through the complex, looking for them.

Dax changed course once more, scooting along on two knees and a hand, holding the tricorder in her other hand. All at once she stopped and turned to face him, inching backward a little more.

She motioned to him, and pointed almost directly downward at the area of ceiling sheet between them.

He pulled up close to her. "Let me go first," he whispered. "Got a few pounds on you."

She nodded, adjusted her phaser, and inched back a little more.

O'Brien holstered his own phaser and flexed his hands. This wouldn't be easy.

Without waiting for fanfare, Dax aimed the phaser and fired directly at the thing they were crawling on.

A pool of red heat spread two feet wide almost immediately, and within seconds there was a gaping hole between them. O'Brien gathered his nerve, shoved his feet through, and jumped, doing all he could to avoid searing himself on the hot edges.

With a shout he plunged onto the floor below, and with his right arm managed to catch the startled Jem'Hadar around the neck. He'd hoped to land square on top of this two-hundred-pound beetlehead, but that's not the way the wheel spun. Luck was with him only in the fact that he landed behind the fellow and not right in his arms. How would that have looked?

The Jem'Hadar practically blew up in O'Brien's arms. It was all the engineer could do to hang on, get his arms around the soldier's throat and hang on for dear life while Dax dropped through the hole after him.

By then, the Jem'Hadar was plunging backward

to pin O'Brien against the wall—oh, yes, that hurt. Half the air was pounded out of him on the first impact, and the Jem'Hadar levered off to do it twice.

O'Brien willed himself to hang on, bury his knuckles in the Jem'Hadar's tough throat plates, and try to cut off his breathing. If he could just weaken the bugger—he felt as if he had a crocodile held up against his body and if he let go he was going to be eaten.

Dax moved in and smashed the soldier across the ribs with the butt of her phaser. There was almost no reaction, except for a brief tuck, then an angry roar. While the soldier clawed at O'Brien's grip on his neck, Dax managed to wrench the energy weapon out of his paw.

The soldier howled with fury. Another purposeful slam, and O'Brien lost his grip.

He fell hard onto his side, arms tingling and numb, his spine rattling, lungs drawing desperately. Forcing himself to act before he lost the chance, he tucked his ribs and coiled both his legs around the Jem'Hadar's ankles just as the big soldier took a grab for Dax to try to get his weapon back.

The Jem'Hadar came down like a felled oak, without the chance to break his fall. The whole deck thrummed.

Staggering onto his knees, O'Brien scrambled to the other side of the corridor, gasping and trying to get the blood back into his trembling hands.

"Stop!" Dax ordered, aiming her phaser and the Jem'Hadar's own energy weapon at him, just in case he didn't understand the phaser. Even if he didn't understand English yet, her message was clear. "Stop! We want to talk to you!"

The Jem'Hadar stopped—just long enough to rip a metal suspension bar off the wall and turn it on O'Brien.

O'Brien ducked at the last second and caught the *whish* of the bar across the side of his head. During the duck, he launched a fist into the Jem'Hadar's face. The good barroom punch gained him about two inches. Enough to slip on past.

But as he dodged, a force came down on the middle of his back as if he'd been struck by a dropping anchor. With a gush of breath he hit the floor on his belly, totally helpless and blinded with pain.

"Stop, I'm telling you!" Dax was calling a few feet away.

O'Brien brought his hands flat on the floor and struggled to push himself up. His legs dangled behind him, numb.

Then, the howl of energy erupted over his head. He ducked and covered his head with both arms. A stink of burning flesh flooded the corridor, and a moment later there was sudden silence.

CHAPTER 7

SOMETHING GRASPED HIS ARM and pulled him over onto his back. He drew back a fist.

"No, Chief, don't!" Dax knelt over him. "I had to vaporize him. He was going to kill you. Are you hurt?"

A grunt of effort helped clear his thoughts as she helped him sit up. "Well, I'm hurting," he groaned. "Big beast just wouldn't give up, would he?"

"No," she said. "Come on. The weapons fire has drawn their attention. I can hear them coming. We've got to get out of here."

She pulled him to his feet. Dizziness swept over him, then a swirl of nausea, but he struggled to straighten up and follow her, as the sound of pounding boots egged him on.

Somehow she found a place for them to hide, where O'Brien could rest for a few seconds. They managed to duck behind—well, there was no telling what it was. Big and black and metal. Good enough.

"Sit down," Dax said to him. She pushed him into a corner, then crouched at guard, phaser drawn, while several Jem'Hadar pounded toward them, past, and right on by.

Sweating like a plow horse, O'Brien clasped an arm over his chest, irrationally afraid the pounding of his heart would summon them here.

After a few moments, Dax scooted backward to huddle with him. "So much for getting one alive."

"Oh," O'Brien gasped, "don't give up yet . . . they're big, but they're dumb. There's a way to corral one."

"How?"

"Well . . . let me get out my . . . my tea leaves and I'll tell you."

Somehow she drummed up one of those smiles again. "All right. Rest."

How could she do that? Smile right in the middle of all this? Without even knowing what happened to the commander and the ship?

O'Brien found Dax's stability heartening, but just another mystery about her. Somehow, in those three hundred years of lifetimes and body-switching, she'd gathered up enough experience to know that nothing's over until it's over and there's always one more wacky thing to try before going down in flames, and even then a stalwart soul could still spit.

"In a minute they'll split up again," she said

quietly, tilting her head and listening to the faint bump of bootsteps through the complex.

Now that his head was clearing and he could breathe again, O'Brien sloughed off his fascination at her coolness and started to grasp at straws. How did a person go about snaring a water buffalo?

"I know!" he began. "Power."

She looked at him. "What?"

"This complex is full of power. Let's use it. We can fabricate some kind of forcefield or numbing field. Not like a phaser blast. Something that would leave our prisoner conscious, but immobilized."

"Tell me what you need."

"I'll need a synthetic or rubber material to insulate myself with . . . and—well, let me hunt about for a minute. Stand guard, eh?"

"Yes, I will."

They moved in two different directions, for two different purposes and one goal.

"Ready?"

"Ready."

"Here he comes."

For the second time in an hour they had isolated a Jem'Hadar soldier moving through the complex by himself. With jolts of phaser noise and tapping on the wall, they'd led him away from the others who were spreading through the area.

Now O'Brien stood beside his improvised zapper field, a monstrous arrangement of electronics cannibalized from the very walls. Except for his nose and his toes, he could just about hide behind it. His right upper arm, wrapped with a rubber gasket, was poised over the enabling hookup.

Down the passageway, Dax stood in full view, rapping her phaser against the wall. It made a hollow thunk.

A guttural shout from another passage gave O'Brien a surge of both victory and terror. They'd attracted another one. Here he came.

Dax let herself be seen, then turned toward O'Brien and ran. Even under these conditions, just for a few seconds, O'Brien couldn't get the image of a gazelle out of his mind.

This new Jem'Hadar came barreling around the corner, howling in rage and joy at having found them.

O'Brien held himself in check as Dax flew past him and his machine—he hoped it would work. There'd been no testing.

As he heard the heavy breathing of the Jem'Hadar and caught the first whiff of the pungent animalistic scent, he threw the switch on his tricorder.

Hooked up to the thing beside him, the tricorder buzzed with effort, and a fierce electric-green field burst to life.

The Jem'Hadar snarled and screamed, but couldn't take another step. A netting of energy caught him by the middle body and dragged him up against O'Brien's mess of crackling equipment. It wasn't working very well, but it was working. Every few seconds it snapped off, then on again, but not enough that the Jem'Hadar could get away.

"Dax! I got him!"

The Jem'Hadar struggled pitifully, thrashing to one side, then the other, pounding the back of his skull against the machines.

Dax ran up to them and stood beside O'Brien, her phaser and energy weapon both trained on the captive, just in case.

"Stop struggling!" O'Brien called to the raging Jem'Hadar, speaking over the rattle and roar of the electrical net. "Stop fighting it! I don't know how much power's going through you. Do yourself a favor, man! Stand still!"

He didn't think it would have any effect and was surprised when it did. The captive slowed his thrashing, as if to see what would happen. The energy net calmed down markedly, but to O'Brien's relief didn't lose all its power. It kept buzzing around the captive, mostly around his chest and neck.

The Jem'Hadar quit struggling altogether, and stood there sucking air, obviously hoping his lack of movement would make the net fade away.

It still might.

Dax glanced at O'Brien, then moved forward. They might not have much time.

"I'm Lieutenant Jadzia Dax from the Federation station *Deep Space Nine,* just on the other side of the wormhole. Do you understand what I'm saying?"

The Jem'Hadar gritted his teeth. Fangs. Whatever those were.

"M'rak!" he said.

O'Brien frowned and looked at Dax. "What d'you suppose that gibberish means?"

The Jem'Hadar flexed his arms and pulled toward him violently. The energy net sizzled hot again and held him. "It's my name!" he boomed.

"Oh . . . sorry."

Dax stepped closer. "We want you to take us to the Founders."

"I will kill you! Or the others will. You will never reach the Founders!"

Raising the energy weapon to their captive's face, Dax firmly said, "We'll kill you if you don't do what we say."

He glowered back at her. "Kill me. I am sworn to guard them. I will *guard* them!"

The field sizzled again, forcing Dax back a step. O'Brien sighed. "This is going well. . . ."

"Why?" Dax persisted. "Why are the Founders so afraid?"

"The Founders are not afraid. They are not for you to see or talk to."

"All right," she said steadily. "Then I will talk to you, and you will listen or we will kill you."

"Kill me."

"No, you listen first. It is your duty to protect the Founders, yes?"

"Yes. Kill me."

"Give it a rest, man, will you?" O'Brien protested as he tampered with his frankenstein machine to keep the power running, and glanced down the corridor, hoping no more Jem'Hadar showed up just yet.

Dax pushed up as close as she could get, so close

that O'Brien could see the fine dark hairs framing her face begin to squirm.

"We're here on a mission initiated by Commander Benjamin Sisko of *Deep Space Nine.* Commander Sisko believes that the Jem'Hadar and the Founders should get a chance at peace before you force us to destroy you. We have fought many wars and never lost. We don't think the Founders understand what is happening. Pay attention to me . . . there is a fleet massing on the other side of the wormhole, awaiting our response. A thousand ships, just like the *U.S.S. Odyssey,* which it took three of your ships to destroy. Do *you* have three . . . thousand . . . ships?"

As she paused and glared into M'rak's face, the captive inched back just enough to give away his shock. He seemed barely able to comprehend that kind of numbers.

"We have weapons that can destroy whole star systems in a single shot," Dax went on.

M'rak made a dirty sound and said, "You lie."

The beautiful woman turned evil before him. "Shouldn't it be up to the Founders to decide?"

Shuddering at the pure venom, O'Brien almost grinned, almost leaned to Dax and told her how well she was doing, but at the last second held himself back. What a crazy thing that would be to do! He must still be half in a daze from that pounding he took. He shut his mouth and admired her in silence as she went on without a flinch.

"Maybe you can win and maybe you can't," Dax said. "But don't you think the Founders should have the choice?"

She stopped talking and stared right into M'rak's astonished face. The glare was one devil of a tactic and she kept it going until O'Brien thought he'd bust.

"If the Founders go to war with the Alpha Quadrant," she went on evenly, "the Founders will be destroyed. That's our message. Don't you think the Founders should hear it?"

M'rak looked at O'Brien, then back at Dax. "The Founders know everything," he protested. "We will protect the Founders. We will destroy you."

"We will destroy the Jem'Hadar," Dax told him without a beat. "And there will be no one left to protect the Founders. And it will be M'rak's fault. *Your* fault."

This time M'rak said nothing, but his face went suddenly numb, as if her message had gotten through his thick skin all at once.

Dax pushed for a vein. "I can prove what I say. And you will protect the Founders by taking us to the Founders."

M'rak narrowed his snakelike eyes. "Prove it."

"All right." Dax stood back a foot or so and holstered her phaser. "I'm going to give you back your weapon now. Chief . . . turn off the field."

O'Brien felt his blood drop to his feet and he almost passed out. He stared at her, waiting for the punch line, but she didn't even look at him.

She continued gazing firmly at M'rak, her purpose fixed in place.

Mourning the thing he'd so quickly fabricated, not to mention his own life, which wasn't going to be ticking along much longer, O'Brien held his breath and turned off the energy net.

The field crackled, gave M'rak a last zap for good measure, then fizzled and died.

Dax held the Jem'Hadar energy gun forward, barrel up.

"I'm giving you this weapon," she gambled. "Kill us if you need to. But remember what awaits our silence."

M'rak blinked down at his hands as Dax placed the ugly weapon into his open paws. The message was even clearer than her extremely clear words. *Kill us and you kill the Founders.*

The Jem'Hadar soldier looked like a big kid holding a firecracker that he didn't know how to light. Evidently Dax had convinced him, at least in part, that he was holding the Founders' future in his hands.

Clumsily fielding M'rak's glare, O'Brien simply shrugged. "You can always kill us later, right?" he contributed.

"Take us," Dax prodded.

M'rak stood straight—and only now did O'Brien notice that this particular monkey stood a good six foot five—and peered down at them like something in a tree. He looked at O'Brien, at Dax, at O'Brien again, and back at Dax. Then he looked down at the weapon in his own hands.

Remember what awaits our silence.

M'rak stumbled sideways and squared off in the middle of the corridor, staring at them.

O'Brien almost drew his phaser, but forced himself to take his cue from Dax.

121

Suddenly M'rak drew a long breath and waved his weapon like a flag, his eyes flaming with fanatical determination.

"I will *take* you!"

He ran off, demanding with his urgency that they follow.

Dax turned in cautious victory to O'Brien. "Let's go, Chief!"

O'Brien hurried along beside her, one hand on his phaser. "You're good at this!" he awarded. "I almost threw up when you gave him that gun back."

"So did I," she said as she stepped up the pace. "And it's not a very pretty picture when a Trill throws up."

M'rak was running full-out, in mortal desperation now to get that message back to the Founders so he wasn't the one who had kept it from them. Simple threat, simply delivered.

To M'rak it was a simple truth and it evidently scared the stuffing out of him. He was almost outrunning them, plowing a path down the narrow corridor.

What a sight we must be, O'Brien thought as he followed Dax at such a run that they almost struck the walls when the path took a turn. He did slam into one outcropping of mechanical stuff and almost got an eye punched out by some odd piece sticking out. This place just wasn't built to have people hurrying through. At least, not people the size of humans, and certainly not the size of Jem'Hadar.

His chest started hurting again as he strained to

keep up. His vision started to close in, turn black on the sides, and he feared he wouldn't be able to stay on his feet. His back knotted and throbbed from the hard punch he'd taken before, and almost everything else hurt too, right down to his ankles. He didn't want to stumble—that would look bad after the show of power Dax had put across.

All at once there was a bloodcurdling commotion before him—he skidded into Dax, and almost instantly she was pulled off him and he was knocked sideways. He skidded to one knee and looked up.

Two more Jem'Hadar!

M'rak had plunged right through them, apparently without noticing them until one of them had reached out and cracked O'Brien a good one.

The engineer stumbled to his feet, but one of the soldiers grabbed him by both arms from behind.

"Run, Dax!" O'Brien scratched his heels against the floor and plowed backward into the Jem'Hadar's chest. For a moment he shoved the soldier off balance, but the grips on his arms never faltered. "Go on, go on!"

The lieutenant's supple posture served well as she communicated through pliancy to the Jem'Hadar soldiers that she was giving up, that she wouldn't fight anymore.

"It's all right, Miles," she said.

He couldn't tell if this was part of the plan she had or just a bet she was making, but she obviously wasn't going to leave him behind.

M'rak came charging back just as the other soldier was leveling his weapon on Dax.

"No!" he shouted. And he started babbling in his own language.

Not a growl of it made a bit of sense to O'Brien. He didn't recognize a single sound or inflection. He'd gotten fair at catching the odd Klingon phrase from time to time and even a word or two of Cardassian, but this was just too new and too snarly to make a bit of sense.

M'rak argued his point fitfully, fanatically, and awfully damned loud. The other two Jem'Hadar stared at him. The one holding O'Brien didn't let go.

Abruptly the other Jem'Hadar, standing between Dax and M'rak, started shouting too, waving his arms and shaking his own weapon furiously.

Then, suddenly and without warning, M'rak leveled his weapon and blasted the guts out of the soldier shouting at him. The soldier choked and tumbled backward, and hit the floor in a gush of his own entrails.

M'rak turned now on the beast holding O'Brien and aimed to shoot.

Dax shouted, "Get down, Miles!"

O'Brien let his body go limp and the surprise of that caused the Jem'Hadar to let go of him in order to defend himself against M'rak. Bands of energy pealed through the corridor as the two had it out right over O'Brien's head, until a heavy body slammed to the floor beside him, crushing one of his legs.

He choked in pain as his pelvis was twisted by the weight of the fallen soldier.

"Chief!" Dax was over him now, shoving the ghastly corpse to one side.

The corridor filled with the stink of Jem'Hadar blood and gore. At the corner, M'rak stood like a colossus, flushed with the panic of his purpose.

"I will *take* you!" he bellowed. "I am *taking* you!"

He waved his weapon in a big beckoning arch, turned, and started pounding away down the passage again, determined to find some other Jem'Hadar who would believe that he had a message to get through.

"Lord," O'Brien gasped. "Is that crackpot going to cut through every one of his own crew like that? We'll never make it! They'll rip us to bits!"

Dax pulled his arm over her shoulders and gave him as much support as she could.

"I've created a monster," she said.

Waxy with sweat, O'Brien forced his bad leg to hold his weight.

Giving her the most encouraging glance he could muster, he straightened his aching back, summoned his voice, and sputtered, "Yes, master—off we go."

Defiant's phasers were thick-beamed flyswatters, power-heavy and extra bright. Aim was fierce and accurate too—one of the Jem'Hadar ships was blown to sparklers with the first shot.

Surprised victory slammed through the bridge, tempered almost instantly by Bashir's hushed voice. They'd hoped the ship could do what she had been designed to do, even unfinished and unfamiliar, and here, for strangers who needed her, she had thumbed her nose at the vicious.

"The other two ships are moving out of phaser range."

"We just gave them something to think about," Sisko said with a flush of vindication, more secure than he felt inwardly. "What's the status of the warp drive?"

T'Rul took an extra second to look up, possibly expecting O'Brien to answer about his own equipment before remembering that he wasn't here and that she was the closest thing to an engineer that they had in their skeletal crew. "The starboard power coupling is completely destroyed. I'm trying to reroute main power."

Sisko glared at her. She'd just told him the sky was falling.

That first shot from *Defiant* had proved that this ship was up to this monumental task, that it could fight to victory, force a peace, or take so many of the Jem'Hadar down that the enemy would be the ones worrying about how to guard the wormhole.

Instead, one of those ships had hammered them a thousand-to-one shot and blown their main coupling! Damn! One lucky shot!

Suddenly they were the *Bismarck* with a smashed rudder, going around in circles while the enemy bore down.

All right, they would die. But they wouldn't die easily.

"They're coming around for another pass,"

Bashir said, "but they're moving a little slower this time."

"They'll be more cautious this time," Sisko bet, hoping the enemy wouldn't realize how crippled he was. "Doctor, use evasive pattern delta-five. We need to keep them off balance until we get warp power back."

"Aye, sir," Bashir responded, eyes on the screen.

One of the Jem'Hadar ships angled into the periphery of the screen, turned on a pylon, and angled toward them on an obvious attack maneuver, weapons slicing across *Defiant*'s bow.

"Torpedoes!" Sisko gasped in that fleeting second between fire and strike.

Around them the ship rocked, then shuddered. On the aft bridge, one of the consoles exploded, sending hot sparks and a putrid electrical stink swelling over the crew.

T'Rul grabbed for a console a full body-length away. "Torpedoes ready."

"Now!" Sisko shouted.

Defiant launched a fan of quantum torpedoes, bright and just as unfamiliar as the weapons of the Jem'Hadar. Each torpedo broke formation and homed in on the nearest Jem'Hadar ship. Instead of the fan opening up, it closed to a spearpoint and all struck at once. If there had been anything in their path, they might have split up and struck two targets, but this time only that one Jem'Hadar ship was within homing range and it had to take the full impact of all those salvos.

Heavy damage sparkled across the enemy vessel. It faltered in its flight path and fell off attack stance.

"T'Rul, where's my warp power?"

Creased with aggravation on the upper deck, T'Rul waved at the smoke still billowing from the exploded panel. "I wish the engines worked as well as the weapons. I can't get the phaser inducers to properly align with the ODN matrices in the—"

"Commander!" Bashir sang out. "Three more Jem'Hadar warships are approaching off the port bow!"

"Full impulse," Sisko said quickly. "Try to get us out of here!"

CHAPTER
8

Disengaged from arms and legs, swimming through open thoughts as detached as snowflakes, Kira Nerys drew a steadying breath.

Consciousness swarmed back with the swelling of her lungs. For a moment all she could think about was a good breakfast and maybe a cold pack for the way her head felt.

Breathe . . . again . . . again.

Dust. Chips of insulation. She coughed. That's what finally roused her. She tried to lift her head.

They still had air . . . no hull breach . . . at least, not in this section. No whistle of leakage.

Wreckage cradled her on both sides. Something must still be falling apart—she heard the crack of metal against metal, chunky wall sections creaking and grinding.

All at once a spasm jumped through her legs and

thighs and her feet started tingling to a point of pain. Circulation had been cut off. Now it was coming back.

She'd been trapped. The noise wasn't more destruction—it was Odo pulling a bulkhead off her.

"Are you all right?" He leaned over her, his long hands scooping under her arms. He helped her to her feet.

She wobbled, but ignored the screaming tingle in her feet and managed to stay up and tap her comm badge. "Just a few bruises. . . . Kira to bridge." Nothing happened. She tried again. "Kira to br—"

The ship rolled again, the deck bluntly dropping away beneath them to port and nearly throwing them both down again. Odo caught Kira's arm and kept her up, and kept himself up by catching hold of an exposed girder that twisted down across the open gap between the berth and the corridor. She almost pulled him back, afraid he would cut his hand on the ragged metal, and only when the ship steadied again did it occur to her that he couldn't *be* cut. The hand could be sliced right off and it would probably jump up, run back, and fuse again.

She shook herself away from that line of thought. "Well, we're definitely in a fight with *someone*. We have to get to the bridge."

He didn't respond, except to start pulling the wreckage away from the hole in the wall so they could both go through.

The corridor was a bastardized memory. Wreckage blocked their way back to the bridge. They were struggling to clear piles of collapsed material and heaps of insulation crumbs when the ship was hit again. They managed to stay on their feet, but the lights went completely out and suddenly they were maneuvering in a collapsed cave.

She felt as if her spine were being compressed. This business of fighting on a ship, dying on a ship . . .

Was the air getting thinner? Was something gushing into the corridors and making her sweat?

They had to get up to the bridge! There she would discover some magic or other that would get them out of this, free her from this enclosing nightmare. She had stared into the face of an enemy who wanted her dead . . . how many times? She had always been able to strike and run, run far. This time, the idea that this ship could be hulled and she and Odo could suffocate or be left for dead, with no power until they froze to death—this was no way to die!

The station had been confining enough for a woman used to the wide spaces of a planet, but at least from the station she could look down and *see* the open areas that had hidden her and her fellow rebels for all the years of her childhood and youth. Not rational, but real.

With a strained flicker, a safety light in the distant corridor came on, casting just enough opaque light for them to make out each other's shapes and the general heap of material they were picking out of their way.

"We've lost main power," Kira said. She still couldn't see her hands. It helped just to hear her own voice.

Odo was moving with nearly frantic determination beside her. "We have to get to one of the shuttles."

"Our duty," she reminded, gauging her tone cautiously, "is to get to the bridge and help defend this ship."

"If main power is out," he said, "then the shields are out too, Kira. There's nothing we can do."

Together they heaved a buckled support knee out of their way.

Kira repressed a shiver. Maybe that was true. Maybe not. Maybe he was glad to have a reason not to struggle to get to the bridge, searching for an excuse to fulfill his drive to get to that place he wanted to go to.

And who was to say the Jem'Hadar wouldn't blast a shuttle to ions?

They *had* to get to the bridge—how could she convince him? How could she let him go flying off into hostile space all by himself?

How could she stop him now?

First they had to get to the end of this corridor. If the whole side of the ship was punched in—

Tall bands of energy hummed before them out of nothing. Pillars of light appeared and formed almost immediately into three Jem'Hadar soldiers.

Do these polliwogs do everything in threes? Kira thought as she charged them. It was the first thing she thought to do, perhaps to catch them in that instant of fog that hits just after transporting.

Within seconds, she was at the throat of a clammy-skinned creature who outweighed her, outgunned her, and outpowered the punch she drew back to throw.

The blow connected with the Jem'Hadar's left eye and he fell back—just long enough for Kira to draw her weapon.

The corridor lit up with phaser fire.

She squeezed again and again, driving one Jem'Hadar behind part of the collapsed bulkhead. She turned in time to see Odo dispatch another of those animals with a blow to the throat.

Counting that as a solid victory, Kira led the way over a metal embankment and landed on the other side of the collapsed inner hull. Recovering, she turned toward the open corridor.

A burst of weapon fire streaked toward her—she thought for an instant that she had squeezed her phaser and fired accidentally—but when the bolt struck her full in the chest, she realized she'd made a mistake.

She'd opened herself to attack . . . if she could get back on her feet, explain her mistake . . . get another chance to aim and fire . . .

Pain poured through her lungs. She battled to stay up, but couldn't tell where up was anymore. Her feet wandered before her eyes, her hands waved in open air. Her head slipped back and she had no more strength to raise it.

The sounds of fighting sizzled away.

"Main power is off-line," T'Rul called over the crackling of the demolished bridge. "The shields have collapsed."

Bashir was coughing. "I've lost . . . helm control
. . . inertial dampers . . . failing—"

"Ready escape pods," Sisko said through a
clamped throat. "Stand by to abandon ship."

They picked through a field of debris, helping
each other across the mess toward the turbolift.

The lights were ninety percent down, the bridge
clouded with chemical smoke from burning consoles. Most of the panels had selectively shut down.
Valiant though she had tried to be, *Defiant* couldn't
hold back the onslaught of so many heavily armed
Jem'Hadar warships.

Sisko clamped his lips and blasted himself for his
foolish attempt to come into this quadrant with
only one ship. Why had he thought any ship could
hold back the Jem'Hadar by itself?

He wanted cooperation, wanted the wormhole to
be used for more than the odd bit of research here
and there, wanted the Bajoran population to know
that Federation membership was more than just a
shipload of antibiotics now and then. He wanted
peace in his life—even if he had to fight for it.

And here he was, barely half a day into the
mission, abandoning their ship, their one chance to
do this.

Two crewmates lost—how many dead here? At
least one engineer here on the bridge. He felt bad
about that young fellow slumped over the helm. He
didn't even know the man's name. How many
belowdecks?

His throat knotted, jaws locked. Dax and
O'Brien—the cost of this failure. He'd botched it
all. Already his mind was racing ahead to the

struggle to get back alive, and after that explaining to Keiko O'Brien and her little daughter that Miles O'Brien was missing, presumed dead . . . and left behind in hostile space.

And what would he go back to? His mission had utterly failed. They had thrown their best punch at the Jem'Hadar and now they would be laughed at. Go ahead, invade, there's no one to stop it from happening.

He was hit with a sudden overpowering urge to get home. Jake needed him. Life was about to become a brutish struggle for survival. He had to be with Jake.

More than that, he had to get back and find some way of keeping these bastards on their own side of the line.

Could he get back in an escape pod?

Limping across space in a pod? With three, six, nine Jem'Hadar ships in the immediate area?

He ushered Bashir up the command-deck steps toward the turbolift. Everyone looked battered. Smoke and hard hits from outside could do that. All their muscles were tense.

Before they even made it to the upper deck, six columns of vibrant energy appeared around the bridge—six Jem'Hadar soldiers materialized, weapons already drawn and raised.

T'Rul was the first to act—she was already armed.

Her disruptor cut through the smoke and stench to slaughter one of the Jem'Hadar at close range.

In retaliation, the nearest to Bashir smashed him across the chest and blew him off his feet, driving him away from Sisko, then moved in for the kill on the helpless physician.

Sisko braced to lunge, but T'Rul came down from the high deck, tackled the Jem'Hadar and slammed to the deck with him, then finished him with two bitter blows to the throat.

Sometimes it was hard to remember that T'Rul was an enemy soldier. Right now it wasn't so hard.

Sisko rounded on another of the Jem'Hadar, but found himself grappling with not one, but two. He twisted and kicked, but he was overwhelmed. These creatures were armored—every blow he delivered landed on a hard, form-pressed surface.

The turbolift blew open and four more Jem'Hadar piled out, spread across the bridge.

Sisko started clawing upward, going for the eyes of the soldiers who held him, but he could barely raise his arms. They had him by both wrists.

So he drove backward and ground an elbow into one of the soldiers' chest plates. There he encountered a measure of give, so he dug his heels into the carpet and rammed harder. Flailing wildly, the Jem'Hadar tripped backward on a fallen chair.

Sisko took it as a gift, cranked around, and buried his fist in the face of the bastard that still had him.

CHAPTER
9

IN ODO'S MIND a piercing demand rang. Not a song, not a call, but it compelled him to answer.

Behind him Kira was down again, hard this time. Dead, probably. She would prefer it to be this way, to die fighting, in one sudden stroke.

It was a chance for him to escape, to shed himself of this part of his life, and go where destiny summoned.

Odo had no feelings for the Jem'Hadar. No feelings. Kira had possessed her own animosity for them and a measure for him. At the moment they were nothing more than an obstacle between himself and the place that called to him. He knew that wasn't right. A few days ago the death of one of his friends would have enraged him. His mind was clogged today.

Escape. The shuttle. He could turn into many

things, some things with no effort, others with such effort that he was left dizzy. He could not turn into his own shuttle and fly away.

As he took his first step around the turn in the corridor that would lead to the shuttlebay, he paused.

She's dead by now. I will surge forward and go where I need to go.

Thus, he had a pretty poor explanation for why he was headed back toward the collapsed corridor. With effort he could split into a million pieces and reassemble again. Then why was it so painful to be pulled in two directions?

He should be used to it. He should be rubber. Oil.

Stumbling over cracked and shattered sheets of wall facing and internal mechanics, he cursed the physical and drove forward through it, constrained by it, drowning in it.

Two Jem'Hadar soldiers roared toward him, brandishing bladed weapons and shouting in a kind of magnificent vanity. One of them had just risen from the dust—and there was Kira, lying beneath the crust of junk where the Jem'Hadar had appeared. Had he killed her?

Yes, she was dead and there was no reason to stay, nothing here for a creature like Odo, no purpose, no way to get to the bridge. He clawed his own fevered mind for an excuse to escape and go his own way.

Destiny boiled in him, but so did devotion. They butted like two fists meeting in midair.

The first Jem'Hadar was almost to him. Odo

stopped moving and stood up straight. All he had to do was laugh and turn and leave.

He kicked at a shattered conduit casing, catching it on his toe and sending it spinning into the first soldier's face. It sliced across his cheek and lodged in his temple. Clutching at the jagged edge, the Jem'Hadar staggered away.

The second soldier was on Odo before the first could gather his agonized howl. Odo had no idea why these two had decided not to use their energy weapons on them—perhaps because Kira was down and they thought they were winning and enjoyed the physical fight.

A day ago this would've been a challenge for him to which he would have clung as a problem in dissecting the intent of the criminal. Today it gave him nothing but a waste of time.

The Jem'Hadar's mouth widened with a snarl of joy as he took Odo's narrow forearm in his own heavy, armored mit and began to twist.

Odo let the creature have a moment's success, perhaps as a tactic or possibly because he was still deciding in which direction he would allow himself to be flung.

Then he caught a glimpse of Kira's iron-red hair lying in a bed of emergency light, and he turned on the Jem'Hadar.

In the Jem'Hadar's grip Odo willed his own arm to melt away. All at once the Jem'Hadar had a handful of liquid and no leverage at all.

Shock threw the Jem'Hadar's eyes backward as he looked wildly for the thing that had just been in his grip.

With his solid hand, Odo brought his elbow back and his shoulder forward and rounded a punch to the enemy's raised chin, and took an instant to enjoy watching the heavy-bodied alien smash into the opposite wall and glare in abject astonishment.

Odo paused and glared back. The Jem'Hadar lay there like a malleted fish and gaped at him, at his own empty paw, then back at Odo.

"Changeling . . . changeling!" the Jem'Hadar gurgled.

While Odo stood over him, the panic-stricken enemy twisted until he gathered his legs, squirmed a body-length away, scrambled up and ran down the corridor, tripped, glanced back, then continued his escape from the terrible monster.

For some reason, Odo found confused satisfaction in that horrified reaction. He let the Jem'Hadar get away and spread the virus of his panic. Where one was afraid, others would hear of the terror.

Besides, he would be gone before the animal found his teeth and came to root him out.

He picked his way back through the wreckage.

Kira wasn't trapped this time. She had taken a hit from the Jem'Hadar energy weapon, possibly the hit that now was saving their lives. The Jem'Hadar had felt secure enough to go into a hand-to-hand fight after Kira went down. They had allowed themselves to savor the fight, and that was their downfall.

Odo filed that tidbit in his memory of how criminals work, and carelessly hoisted Kira out of the rubble.

Now—*now*—finally he could plunge full into those other desires, go where this inner pounding demanded he go.

Kira moaned against him as he carried her to the shuttlebay, but this was her only protest, and this he could ignore.

The shuttlebay was arctic cold and pressure was dropping. There was a structural breach somewhere. Slow leak. Every wall was crusted with moisture gradually turning to ice. As he arranged Kira in the copilot's seat, Odo began to worry that the bay doors would jam and he still would be trapped here, an inch from death with this knelling in his head that insisted he go off into unknown space and find the bell.

"Computer," he rasped as he dropped into the pilot's seat. "Launch sequence."

"Acknowledged," the dead-toned voice responded. "Engines on. Life support activated. Shuttlebay depressurizing."

"Sensors scan immediate area and report."

"Scanning . . . registering twelve vessels over one hundred thousand tons each, no coordinated formation, seven within shuttle phaser range."

"Shields up. Stand by phaser weapons. Red Alert. Open shuttlebay doors."

Before him on the wide screen, the huge fluted bay doors began to open like an Oriental fan. He paused for that moment during which he could do nothing else and absorbed his last view of this technical life he had led. The shuttlebay doors jarred for a few seconds, then continued to open, but that pause shook him out of his reverie.

Beyond the doors, he could see three . . . four
. . . five of the Jem'Hadar ships. One was maneuvering away and turning to approach again. Others
were holding a pattern, and at least one was adrift.

"Emergency launch, battle mode," he said sharply, as though that would help.

The computer forced all systems to immediate
heat, and the shuttle surged out of the bay at twice
normal launch speed.

Two of the Jem'Hadar ships tried to fire on the
shuttle immediately, but couldn't turn fast enough
to take a fix on a target shooting out of the back of
the pounded *Defiant.* For some reason these idiots
failed to anticipate launch of any life pods or
shuttles. Either that, or they simply didn't know the
design of Federation ships and didn't know where
the launch bay was.

Could they be so stupid?

Odo glanced at Kira, still slouched in the copilot's seat, and wished she were awake to help him
appreciate the enemy's dullness of wit. He thought
again of how the Jem'Hadar had run away from his
shapeshifting abilities, and reveled that his last
action in this concrete life he had lived would be
one of such pure simplicity. These were creatures of
the concrete.

He could use that.

A science shuttle was no fighter. It wouldn't even
have the maneuverability of a station runabout. In
a few seconds, his element of surprise would be
completely gone. The two Jem'Hadar ships that
had fired and missed were even now spreading the
word that there was a shuttle escaping.

He thought about asking the computer to plot locations of all the other ships, but he didn't care about those. He would deal with the ships he could see, and then he would get through them and go as far away as anyone had ever been.

The *Defiant* had apparently had a vicious and striking effect, he realized as he surveyed the five ships—six now—that he could see. At least three were definitely limping, one completely adrift.

"Computer, scan the drifting ship for life-forms."

"Scanning . . . no life-forms. Ship is completely depressurized. There are signs of toxic chemical leakage."

Hull breach, both inner and outer. The crew had been poisoned first, then suffocated. The same fate he had feared might happen to *Defiant* had been foisted upon her enemy.

Again he wished Kira could see. In the coming hours, when he was forced to tell her that the ship was abandoned and there was no sign of other life pods, no rational suggestion that the commander or any of the others might have survived, she would need something to cling to.

He was assuming they would survive the next few minutes.

The shuttle selectively dodged another shot from one of the limping ships and Odo was forced to catch Kira as she was nearly pitched out of her seat. Realizing he should've laid her amidships where she would be safer, he pushed her back and took over control from the computer. Though he daily refuted the concrete, today he wanted to have his hands on the controls, to make the shuttle do his bidding, and land one personal blow before he resigned himself to seclusion.

The swarm of Jem'Hadar ships were turning on him now, though the shuttle could maneuver better in tight space than the large ships. Good—the Jem'Hadar hadn't thought to launch any smaller sweeper vessels for just this kind of emergency.

He didn't want to fight them. He wanted to get away, to fly toward that ringing in his head and the place on the star chart that had set off the alarm.

Another ship moved in below him. They were boxing him in. He angled sharply to sub-starboard and suddenly there was a rain of debris whacking and pounding the shuttle's shields. Odo leaned forward to see what was hitting the shuttle, and noted several manufactured parts fly past. Parts of a ship, a completely shattered vessel.

The *Defiant* had done even better than he had realized.

Parts of a ship—as dangerous as asteroids.

He turned sharply again and dipped into the drifting field of debris, bumping and slamming his way through, and two of the ships pursuing him slowed down to contemplate what they should do.

The debris field got thicker, more dangerous. The shuttle bumped past many sharp edges and broken pieces that could impale the shuttle in an instant, but he couldn't think of that.

He shouldn't have brought Kira. If the shuttle was destroyed, he might survive. He wasn't like her. He might find some way to cling to something. . . .

But she was here and her life was in his hands. For her to survive, the shuttle had to survive.

When he saw a clear area of space, clear but for the derelict Jem'Hadar ship with no life aboard, he headed out of the debris field and took a direct course for the dead ship. Two other Jem'Hadar vectored into pursuit. In seconds they would be in firing angles.

Another ship came up under him again. His hand hovered over the phaser-enable . . . if he could hold back a few seconds . . .

The dead ship loomed on his forward screen. Increase speed toward it . . . hold course . . .

Bolts of energy surged up from below his forward viewport. The nearest ship was firing on him—and missed. They wouldn't miss again.

Closer to the derelict ship, closer . . . target its weakest points, where *Defiant* had already ruptured the hull braces.

"Fire," he uttered aloud, and hit the enable.

Phasers lanced from the shuttle to the dead ship and cut cleanly across the nose and into the blaster ports. The dead ship split along its damage lines and fell apart, ripping its own power feeds to bits.

When the pressurized fuel cells were sliced open, they blew up. A great red plume vomited across the space before him.

The shuttle was pummeled and sent spinning, but since it was already past the ship it was sent along its own trajectory and simply pushed away.

"Aft viewer," Odo ordered, and looked at the monitors.

The ship behind him was drowned abruptly in the explosions from the crippled vessel. Since the Jem'Hadar had been in pursuit of him, it had been heading directly toward the derelict vessel and hadn't vectored off in time.

He paused and watched. Glittering damage blew along the length of the pursuing ship as it hit the fusion reactions blowing out of the dead vessel. The raw power it took to bring life into space could also turn upon life and destroy it.

Satisfaction could find no harbor, though, for immediately there were two more Jem'Hadar angling to fire on him.

He was forced to turn off his course, away from the bell in his head. There was no path to get away, except to go between the ships that were turning toward him.

Death at the hands of the Jem'Hadar—his legacy. A legacy instead of a destiny. His and the major's together.

And no one would ever know. He had left no log, nor could he take time to leave one now.

That was bad judgment. Inefficiency. He should have taken that time.

The Jem'Hadar ships were positioning to head him off now. He could see the glow of gathering power in their weapons ports.

Leaning forward as though to urge the shuttle onward, he increased speed again, preparing to run the gauntlet. Run it and die.

The Jem'Hadar ships were enormous from this vantage point, great ambling fortresses in space, bottles of unthinkable power and alien design.

They were almost angled to slaughter him, to fire on him without getting in each other's crossfire.

A glowing weapons port destroyed his appreciation for the massive picture gathering before him.

He pushed the speed. The two ships grew huge before him, one on the side, one on top. With one hand on the console, he reached to his side with the other hand and placed it over Kira's arm, as if to hold her in her seat as they died. What else could he do to preserve her last instant of dignity?

Humans liked to close their eyes at moments like this. He had seen some of them do it.

He had no urge to close his eyes.

The two ships turned a little more toward him as his shuttle raced at blinding speed toward the sliver of space between them. Beyond them, another enemy ship was maneuvering.

Suddenly he leaned forward and let go of Kira. What had he seen?

The weapons portals were falling cool. Cease fire?

No—he must be imagining it!

Why would they?

The shuttle soared between the two Jem'Hadar ships, then onward to the one waiting beyond, and then miraculously beyond that.

He twisted to look at the aft viewer, to see if they were trying to hit his thruster ports, but that didn't make sense. Those ships could cut this shuttle apart with one swipe, without the slightest aim.

They weren't maneuvering to pursue. In fact, they were coming to all-stop behind him. He was beyond them!

They had ignored him. Considered him inconsequential. Given him up to those depths of space. Did they know something about this area of space that he didn't know? Were they laughing, because there was nowhere for the fool in the shuttle to go in such a small ship?

Sagging in the seat, Odo faced forward again and found his limbs trembling.

Vibrating around him, the shuttle continued to race outward now, heading into the depths of black space, farther than anyone from the Alpha Quadrant had ever ventured.

He had escaped. He had saved Kira.

Now he would save himself.

CHAPTER
10

AIR ... WARM AND QUIET. No pounding. No smell of burned insulation. The subliminal hum of engines.

A moan. Her own—and a faint buzz in her throat. Elbows against padding ... she pressed back on them.

And she almost fell out of the seat.

With heavy concentration Kira managed to open her eyes.

Before her, a helm/navigation control board. A runabout?

No. This was a Starfleet shuttlecraft cockpit.

She shoved her head forward, insisting that her neck muscles do their work. They did, but it hurt.

"Where am I?"

"You're in a shuttlecraft. You've been wounded, so try not to move around much."

With a wince, she looked to her side. Odo was piloting the shuttle.

She touched a tender spot on her temple and tried to judge just how badly she was wounded.

Memory flooded back and she grasped for the control board to hold herself upright. "Odo, what happened? The *Defiant* . . . the Jem'Hadar—we were under attack!"

Odo never took his eyes off the console. "The ship was boarded and you were wounded in the attack. I managed to get us to a shuttlecraft, but I don't know more than that. The last time I saw the *Defiant* she was dead in space and surrounded by Jem'Hadar ships."

"Sisko?" she gasped. "Bashir?"

"I don't know."

Resistance volleyed through Kira's aching head. She soaked in the shock and tried to deal with the crashing thoughts of her commanders and her shipmates, her friends, caught up in the Jem'Hadar web. How many had they left behind? Until now she hadn't even tried to count up the number of skeleton crew they'd put on board. O'Brien had been in charge of that. How many engineers had been belowdecks? Not many . . . two or three, maybe. How many on the bridge? One?

Had they escaped, or were they all still back there, fighting?

"Where are we?"

"Approaching the Omarion Nebula."

She twisted to him no matter how much it hurt. "You should have taken us back to the wormhole."

"You didn't object at the time."

"I was unconscious!"

"Your most cooperative state."

Through the main viewer, the Omarion Nebula lay like spilled paints across the black matte of space. Arms of the nebula reached out and spilled around the shuttlecraft. They were already inside it.

Cloying worry struck her. This wasn't Odo. To leave the others without checking about their condition . . . and to fail to take vital information back to the Alpha Quadrant that might never be known if the two of them didn't survive? Not Odo at all.

He didn't even seem particularly concerned with her.

No, that couldn't be all there was. Something was working on him, driving him in the wrong direction. His hands on the controls, the fixed expression on his face—and he wouldn't look at her.

"All right," Kira relented. "Have you found anything?"

He didn't answer. But by the set of his hands and body, the stern unrest in his eyes, he hadn't seen anything yet to make him turn back. He was still magnetized by whatever force had moved him to come here.

Just when she thought he wasn't going to respond at all, he nodded slowly, without looking at her.

She shifted to look at his monitor.

"There's a class-M planet ahead . . . but no star system. A rogue planet?"

"Yes," he said, deep in his rapture.

Unwilling to settle for murmurs, Kira pressed,

"You think that planet is what you've been looking for?"

Somehow the bluntness of her demand seemed to surprise Odo. He fielded a moment of wonder, thrill, panic, then clearly fought to get those reactions out of his face.

"I'm going to find out," he said.

A darkened planet, roaming through space, unescorted by the most meek of debris.

Wide and broad though outer space might be, rare was the body that ran alone. This was one.

No home star brightened the surface of this place. Only the charitable haze of distant clusters and the wash of comets' tails lay a moonlike gauze over the surface.

The choppiness of coming through the crystal clear atmosphere left Kira nauseated. Probably the head injury, she decided as she waited for her eyes to adjust to the constant twilight here.

Odo had set the shuttle down in a small clearing where sensors had read a quiet forest area. Over there was a broad lake, sprawled over a marshy area, rolling and surging as if there were wind here.

But there was no wind.

Forest . . . atmosphere . . . lake . . . on a planet with no sun? No heat source?

It had taken Kira until now to realize how impossible that was and assimilate that there was something more spooky about this place than just purple shadows and branches breathing against the sky. The fact that they could land here, breathe here—it went against everything she had ever learned during her tenure in space.

Forever night. This was a mournful place.

The two wandered together pointlessly, trying to find something with their senses, their experience, and their bald curiosity. Kira followed Odo, hoping the instinct that had brought him here would also give him direction now.

Was Odo a lower life-form or a higher one than herself and her own people? Or something completely different, not on the line of evolution so many humanoids had traversed?

Of course, he only appeared humanoid as a matter of convenience, or perhaps to fit in. He really did want to fit in, she knew, and that was the root of her affection for him. Hers, Quark's, Sisko's . . .

The commander—where was he? And Julian and the rest. Captured? Held by the Jem'Hadar? Would torture come into the picture?

Leading the way toward the polished lake, Odo moved through crisp waving grasses that clung to his long legs and danced with reeds whose heads bobbed in the starlight.

The lake responded to the starlight, rolling and moving in imaginary winds. Drenched in fatigue and the lingering aches of her wounds, Kira wanted to sit down beside the reeds and watch them, lie down beneath the stars and the sweeping arms of the nebula overhead and to all sides, and watch the liquid in the lake move and sway.

Liquid . . . why hadn't she thought "water"?

She stopped walking and scanned the lake as Odo approached the edge.

He looked down into the gleaming mercurial brew as if looking at a mirror. He did all but stoop down and touch it, though he seemed throbbing to do so.

Kira watched him.

She was still watching him when the lake started to move—and then she watched the lake.

Pillars of gelatin rose from the edge of the lake. Purposefully they formed into four humanoids, their faces and bodies the same unfinished plastic of Odo's face, simple tunics draped from their shoulders.

Kira wanted to step back, withdraw from the moment, but she was too stunned to move.

Some were female, some male, all gazing with unmeasurable sensation at Odo, who stood staring back.

A female creature smiled and came toward Odo. She parted her narrow lips and blinked her nymphlike eyes.

"Welcome home," she said.

CHAPTER
11

IN THE LILAC HAZE of the nebula's arms above, the lakeshore swelled and fell back, then did the same again, as though tasting the gentle grasses, which would not be able to grow anywhere but on a magical world, if that world had nothing but starlight with which to nourish them.

There was no sun here to nourish them, yet they grew. No warmth, yet they flourished.

Kira Nerys watched all this through her throbbing eyes, demanding that this not be a dream inflicted by her injuries, and she knew it wasn't. Beside her the mysterious and melancholy Odo, always privately desolate, grieving relations he had never known, was today standing on the brink of fulfillment. He had found others like himself.

The other shapeshifters looked just like him. That same premanufactured doll face, like a doll before the features were painted, or a doll caught for a moment in a fire. A face that just wasn't finished.

Were they doing that on purpose?

Kira tried to think like these creatures, but empathy had never been her strong suit. Survival, but not empathy.

Were these creatures trying to empathize with one of their own kind? They hadn't imitated her face, so they didn't have any doubt which one of the two was their kind. She'd seen Odo make the detailed faces of rats and other living things, and she'd seen subtle improvements in his imitation of the human form, so she assumed there were shapeshifters here who could do better or worse if they had the skill.

Yet they were mirroring his image, his version of this form.

Could it be that they hadn't seen any better version than his?

But I'm standing right here ... they must be doing this for him. A kind of welcome ...

Odo stood in some kind of shock beside her, staring at the four shapeshifters, who simply stared back as if they'd give him all the time in eternity and had it to give.

"You really are just like me," he croaked ultimately, "aren't you?"

"Yes," the female shapeshifter in the foreground said.

"And ... this is where I'm from?"

"This is your home."

He swallowed a few lumps, scanned the beautiful lake of mercury, and seemed afflicted to accept what he saw.

"I wish I could remember it."

"It's understandable that you cannot. You were still newly formed when you left us."

He took an imperceptible step toward her. "Newly formed? You mean I was an infant?"

"An infant, yes."

Kira peered through the gauzy starlight, trying to read the masklike face of the being who spoke, detecting an unfamiliarity with that idea—infant. This creature was doing everything she could to understand what Odo was talking about and provide him with the answers that had been his constant torment in the past.

Odo steeled himself for the big question, and had less trouble than Kira would have predicted in asking it.

"Tell me—do I have parents? Any family at all?"

"Of course," the shapeshifter said. Behind her, the three others stood in mute support.

"I'd like to meet them," Odo requested, "if that's possible."

The shapeshifter motioned to the others, and to the big lake. "You already have. We are all part of the great link."

Before them all, the lake moved and surged, as though responding, knowing she was talking about it . . . them.

Odo peered out at the lake. "Is that all of us, or are there others?"

DIANE CAREY

Kira looked at him. He was having such trouble dealing with the whole situation—he'd reverted to courtroom questions, probably that had been festering in his mind for a long time. She had no idea how long.

Suddenly she felt a little guilty for knowing so little about him.

"Odo," she murmured, "this isn't a police investigation."

"I'm aware of that, Major," he grumbled back, but there was a twinge in his posture that hinted gratitude.

"Then stop interrogating these people," she pursued. "You've waited your whole life for this moment. The least you can do is try to enjoy it." She moved forward toward the edge of the lake and the four lissome shapeshifters standing like angels in the starlight. "He really is happy to be here . . . aren't you?"

"Yes, of course," he stammered, and seemed embarrassed that he had communicated something else. "It's just . . . this is all very sudden—"

"And you have many questions," the female said, smiling.

Bolstered by her gentle anticipation, Odo said, "Yes."

"I wish we could answer them all for you. Unfortunately we find the language of the solids to be as imprecise and awkward as their bodies."

Irritated, Kira found the shapeshifter's bluntness rude, but decided to ignore that if she could get clarity. "Solids?" she asked.

The bland face turned to her. "Our term for

158

monoforms like yourself who will never know the joy of the great link."

Maybe it was an insult, but Kira didn't really care about that. Something in their attitude was making her stomach tight. An arrogant disregard for her personal identity? Her very existence? Yes, that was it. They didn't just regard her as unimportant, but as inconsequential. That female entity looked at her with the same cold-bloodedness as a thousand Cardassians she'd encountered in her life.

"Well, Odo has *had* to communicate with us, and he hasn't done too badly."

"I doubt Starfleet Command would agree with you, Major," Odo said.

The female shapeshifter waited until he looked at her again. "Have you enjoyed living among the solids?" she asked.

"At times . . . though I never really felt at home with them."

"What exactly," Odo asked, "is this great link you keep mentioning?"

Kira almost stammered an answer before noticing that he wasn't talking to her.

Odo was still squared off with the female of his own kind.

"The link is the foundation of our society," the female said. "It provides a meaning to our existence. It is the merging of form and thought, the sharing of idea and sensation."

Kira watched Odo digest these vaguenesses. At first she couldn't understand why he didn't plunge in. Literally.

But as she watched him, she realized how foolish that would be, even if it's what she would have done. It was the mistake she always made—that somehow a physical similarity meant people were the same.

She'd assumed that before and she'd been wrong.

After a life of solitude, the prospect of imminent merging was overwhelming for Odo. He faced the opening of everything he had ever felt, decided, thought, to the scrutinization of strangers.

Yes, these beings were only strangers, as if Kira herself had been dropped in a tub with a thousand Bajorans she had never met. That must be what was troubling Odo—likeness didn't necessarily mean sameness.

What was their way of life, their common measure of rights and wrongs? Fluid of physical nature though he might be, Odo was used to dealing with the intensely concrete. Day by day he had dealt with the brutal inflictions of the Cardassians and Jem'Hadar, the latter of which might today have cost the lives of their closest associates and the man whose orders were the anchors of all their days. He had gone from the grip of the Cardassians to the slingshot freedom of the Federation. He knew all the grandeurs and pettinesses of a gurgling civilization, but he didn't know this commonality, this "link" his own kind talked about.

She saw that he was smart enough to understand that he didn't know. He was holding back. Yes, that was smart. Even more, it was wise.

Her admiration of him ratcheted up a couple of notches.

Once again the female gestured at the vast silver swarm.

After trying to swallow all this talk about merging and sharing, Odo scoped out more answers by saying, "It sounds very . . . intimate."

Kira could tell he wasn't trying to be polite. He was trying to get a clearer explanation.

The female shapeshifter smiled pliantly at him again. "That is an adequate description."

So the language wasn't so bad, so inaccurate, after all, Kira noted. She knew Odo hoped there would be more.

"It's just," he faltered, "I've lived a very solitary life."

"That was unfortunate," the womanlike form said, "but necessary, as you'll learn in time. But that part of your life is over. You're home."

She extended her hand. Nearby, a male shapeshifter reacted to the gesture. "What are you doing?" he asked.

"Take my hand, Odo," the female said.

The male moved forward a little. "But it's not time. He isn't ready."

The female looked only at Odo. "He has been gone too long. He needs to remember, if only for a moment. Don't be afraid," she said to Odo. "Take it."

With less hesitation than Kira expected, Odo reached out and clasped the female's hand.

Together, the two hands blended into the silvery satin of their natural state and glowed mauve under the deep shadows and ashy night.

Odo's face lost its tension, his eyes their focus. Kira thought for a moment that he would slip away, be drawn into that gunmetal mass, and she would never be able to get him back. He was so vulnerable right now, could he think for himself in that liquid state? What did it mean for him to be swallowed by that opal mass?

Where would his mind go when he was in there?

She couldn't comprehend that kind of existence and suddenly didn't want to try. They were here and Odo was here, she was here and all she wanted was for all this to work out. She wanted to go home just as much as she wanted Odo to find his real home.

Almost immediately the female broke the grasp. Their two shapeless forearms warbled briefly in the liquid state, then drew into human hands again.

The female looked satisfied. Odo, though, looked as if he'd been hypnotized.

"Odo?" Kira attempted. "Odo?"

He didn't respond. Just stood there, dazed.

"What did you do to him?" she asked the shapeshifter, trying not to sound accusative.

"I allowed him to experience the link."

Kira ignored the repeat of vagueness, reached over, and clasped Odo's arm. "Odo . . ."

He blinked, turned to look at her, and finally said, "Yes, Major."

"Are you all right?" She gave him a moment to nod, then asked, "What happened?"

He blinked at her before looking again at the

wide lake, its shimmering oyster surface that moved with inner momentum, and at the beings who waited in perfect simplicity for his decision.

Rare proof shone in his face. He was smiling.

"I'm not sure," he said. "But I know one thing. They're right . . . I'm home."

CHAPTER
12

"COMMANDER'S LOG, SUPPLEMENTAL . . . It's been six days since we were forced to abandon the *Defiant* during the Jem'Hadar attack. We still don't know what happened to the rest of the crew. Dr. Bashir and I have plotted a course back to the wormhole, but whether our shuttle can get us there is questionable. Our engines are failing, our external sensors are barely functioning, and life-support systems are at twenty percent and dropping."

"But other than that, we couldn't be in better shape."

Julian Bashir's voice startled Ben Sisko as he tried to make his log entry without disturbing the doctor.

In the copilot's seat beside Sisko, Bashir straightened up and smiled at him.

"I thought you were sleeping," Sisko said apologetically.

He'd waited until Bashir fell asleep to begin his roster of all things broken and cracked, all possibilities fading fast, and hadn't mentioned in his log that their visual and audio communications were out, most of the monitors busted, and the escape pod's thruster ratios off-line because of the battering the little ship had taken in the asteroid belt.

He tried not to grumble too much about the asteroids that had saved their lives. Trying to back-alley fistfight away from the half-dozen Jem'Hadar who'd stormed the bridge was a losing adventure, but he'd tried it anyway. Something inside him had just refused to give up and try to "negotiate" his way out of the moment. Those creatures hadn't been out to talk. They'd been out for blood. Hand them the sword, and they'd have hacked him and Bashir to death with it.

He'd seen Bashir go down, valiantly kicking, and felt himself draining of strength after investing most of his knuckles in at least four Jem'Hadar faces, and he thought he'd been hit when the *Defiant* shuddered over and over around them.

Asteroids—big ones, little ones, iron-compound ones, wonderful ones. In a complete panic, the Jem'Hadar had rushed back to their ships before the rain of rocks pulverized them. The low-level grunts who had stormed *Defiant*'s bridge had been stupid enough to run for cover without their captives. They thought they were leaving Sisko and Bashir to die on the condemned starship.

In the confusion, bare minutes before *Defiant*

was hammered to slivers, Sisko pushed Bashir into an escape pod and blasted out while the shuttlebay collapsed behind them.

An escape pod—just small enough to dodge the medium and large asteroids and duck out of sensor range of the Jem'Hadar. Just sheer luck he hadn't piled into one of those rocks while trying to remember how to fly one of these walnuts.

"From the sound of things," Bashir said, "I wish I *were* still sleeping."

"Things could be worse," Sisko told him, remembering the jar of asteroids piercing the starship's hull plates as he dragged Bashir through the ship.

He was lying. Things could be worse, but not much more horrible. He hadn't been able to find Kira or Odo. Hadn't even been able to reach those decks.

He hadn't even known where Bashir had quartered Odo—didn't even know where to look. Sensors had been down . . . only their two lives . . . that was all he had been able to salvage with his bruised hands and his pitiful efforts.

And how often could that happen to one man, and have him remain sane?

His heart still pounded to go back when he thought of them, even after six days. How could he ever know now whether the *Defiant* was destroyed by the asteroids, cut apart in vengeance by the Jem'Hadar, brought in tow like a miserable hulk and hauled back so those bastards could take credit for damage they didn't complete, or whether his shipmates were trapped inside, to be tortured or killed?

How could he have left without knowing?

For the second time in his life.

In someone else's life.

No regulation in his fleet or any could fault him, yet his heart roiled.

And now the only succor, the only armor of wisdom, he could give his one remaining companion was to say that things could be worse. Marvelous.

He poked at a few controls. Didn't help.

Suddenly the pod slammed to a dead stop, throwing them both forward hard.

"I believe you!" Bashir gasped, clinging to the arms of his chair, his face once again sheeted white.

Sisko pushed himself back from his panel and checked it. "We're not moving."

"You think it's some kind of tractor beam?"

"Could be . . . I wish these sensors were working."

The ship was hit again, this time with a sonorous metallic clang that echoed inside. Somebody had a mighty big can opener.

"Now what?" Bashir yammered.

Sisko listened to the scrapes and understood their verdict.

He pushed out of his chair and pulled his phaser. Heartfelt pride bubbled past his panic when Bashir also pushed forward to the hatchway and drew his own weapon. A blunt sensation washed through Sisko that his crewmates were too good for him. He couldn't let Bashir down as he had let down the others.

This whole mission—such folly! Fly into hostile space and demand that it cease hostility, that it see the broad future that could be before them as clearly as he saw it, so no one else would ever have to abandon their friends, their crew, their families in the heat of battle, and doubt for the rest of their lives.

It *wasn't* folly, he insisted as he leveled his phaser at throat height on the hatch. Safety and peace were things to be constructed and insisted upon, not to be hoped for while quivering in a dark corner. Anyone who thought the Alpha Quadrant could be safe while that wormhole remained open—and how long would that be? Two weeks or two million years? There was no real isolation anywhere.

He wanted that safety and the flourishing that could come with it. Wanted it for his son and all the others trying to carve out a life on the edge of the new frontier.

"Wait until you have a clear shot," he said to Bashir.

The doctor squared his phaser on the hatch and arranged his feet squarely on the cramped, contoured deck. "Right."

Sisko fixated on that hatch, driven daft by the clanging and clunking going on out there. All right, so the hatch was jammed. So what? Torch it open and get on with it. Waiting for a fight was always the worst part of the fight.

How many would come through there? The first two would be phasered down for sure. After that, one or two more might be hit again if both he and Bashir were fast enough to get shots in before they were shot at.

How was the entranceway to the ship that was boarding them? How deep? Could more than two charge in at a time? Calculations raged through his mind even as adrenaline tried to drum them out and make him revert to instinct, punch his way out without a plan. The punching might work, as it had on *Defiant,* but he wanted the plan just in case.

If they came in shooting—

Boom . . . There it was. Docking.

The hatch shuddered, creaked. Began to slide open against its own dented frame.

Sisko stiffened his hand on the phaser. He was one pulse beat from etching his name in the metal, not even waiting until he saw a face come through.

Good thing he waited. The face that came through was O'Brien's.

"Hold on! What kind of a greeting is that?" the engineer said quickly. "Don't shoot! We surrender."

And Dax's face too—

"Chief!" Sisko surged. "Dax!"

Bashir almost tripped on his own relief. "I don't believe it! We thought you'd been captured by the Jem'Hadar!"

Breathing heavily just from having to stand there and wait to shoot, Sisko lowered his phaser with specificity, knowing his hand was still so cramped on that trigger that he could hardly feel his fingers.

Dax looked at him, then at Bashir, with that bright-eyed non-smile, with just the corners of her lips drawn outward slightly, as if she thought they were cute or something. "We had our doubts about ever seeing you again either, Julian."

O'Brien nudged Bashir's phaser a little more down and said, "We've been searching for you for days."

Sisko nodded, suddenly impatient. "What about the others?"

Dax lowered her eyes briefly, then brought them back up again, and they weren't exactly pools of hope.

"No sign of them yet," she said. "But we still have ships out looking for them."

"Meanwhile," O'Brien added, "our orders are to get you back to DS9 as soon as possible."

Dax took Sisko's arm and angled him toward the open hatchway. "Big things are going on there, Benjamin. I think you're in for a surprise."

A brilliant sky. The paint of night inside a nebula.

Of night forever.

Moss-velveted rocks, rustling ornamental grasses, broad hosta leaves bowed in the changeless starlight. Ivy, fern, ribbongrass, reeds, tufts of sedum, lamb's ears, moonflower, and stargazing lilies punctuated a perfectly formed meditation garden. There was even something that looked like bamboo, and over there flowering tobacco and herbs added gentle scents.

Rocks and benches broke through the tranquility to add texture and encourage pause.

Still weakened and aching some, Kira paused

over a clump of what looked like some kind of ornamental cabbage. The first-aid kit in the shuttle had provided antibiotics, some high-powered analgesics, and a couple of stimulants, all designed to give a wounded person a boost in an emergency situation, which was the general idea behind the first-aid kit—assuming a person using it might need strength and consciousness more than rest.

But she still ached. She turned and looked at the sky, disturbed by knowing that there wasn't— would never be—sunlight to make these fronds grow. All this was false. Not just sculpted and groomed, but flat-out fabricated. This was the most purposeful garden she'd ever seen.

Nearby, Odo was oblivious to the draped and rustling beauty around him . . . beauty that might have been created *for* him. She wasn't ruling out that possibility. Just because they found the planet didn't mean they hadn't been expected. They obviously knew *something* about Odo.

He wasn't looking at anything in the garden. He sat, alone of spirit, a few paces away and stared at the distance as if expecting some unplanned arrival.

Kira wandered back toward him. "Whoever created this place was a real artist. It's beautiful."

"How long do they plan on making us wait here?" was the edgy response.

Not getting too close, Kira said, "It's only been a few hours."

"I finally return home and I'm still treated like an outsider."

"Believe me," she told him, "you're not the outsider here. I am."

He looked at her. "You?"

"You heard the way they talked about 'solids.' I'm the one they don't trust. Not you."

She started to say more, to apologize to him for casting suspicion on him in the eyes of his own kind, but another voice cut through her intent.

"How perceptive of you, Major."

They both turned, Odo with cautious anticipation, Kira with some physical effort. The female shapeshifter was entering the garden behind them.

"If our history has taught us anything, it's to be wary of solids," the creature said.

Kira drew up her posture and squared her shoulders. "That may be, but I think you'll find Odo's done quite well living among us."

The female looked at Odo. "Is this true?"

"I'd say that on the whole it has been gratifying," Odo condensed.

"But as you say, you've never really felt at home with them," the female said. "That's because your home is with us." She turned to Kira. "Unfortunately, I can't say the same about you. We have no place for you here."

Kira dropped her attempt at pride and went straight for bluntness. "I don't intend to be staying long." She turned to Odo and added, "There's still a chance Sisko and the others could have survived the attack. I'll try contacting them from the shuttle."

"I'm sorry." The shapeshifter moved her hands uneasily. "We cannot allow any communications to be sent from the planet's surface. They could be traced back here. We value our isolation."

"Yes, of course," Odo said.

The female nodded to Kira. "However, you're free to leave here to search for your friends at any time."

Gratified that the shapeshifter had at least avoided saying something deprecating about "solids" again, Kira simply said, "If you don't mind, I think I'll stay a while longer."

If the supple alien did mind, it didn't show. "As you wish. However, you'll have to provide your own shelter and provisions, as we lack those essentials necessary to sustain humanoid life."

"Don't worry about me. I'll be fine."

The female gave another nod, this one more dismissive, and turned again to Odo.

"I hope you've made good use of our arboretum."

Perplexed, Odo asked, "In what way?"

"By assuming the various shapes and life-forms surrounding you."

Odo glanced at Kira. For a moment she thought he was going to ask *what* life-forms, but he asked, "Why would I do that?"

"Isn't it obvious? To become a thing is to know a thing. To assume its form," the female proposed, "is to understand its existence."

"Understand it? How?"

The female surveyed him as if he had the question engraved across his bare brow. Sadness and pity weighed her gaze.

"Living among the solids," she said, "has damaged you far worse than I realized. It has left you ignorant of the gifts you possess."

Kira wrinkled her nose to avoid opening her mouth. *So if I put on an egg crate, does it make me an egg? Do these people believe that form is more important than substance? No wonder they don't understand us.*

Unfortunately, Odo suddenly looked humbled, even shamed. "Then teach me what I need to know," he said.

The female nodded slowly. "I will do what I can. But in the end, this is another journey you must make on your own. And when it's over, you will be ready to take your place in the great link."

She reached into a bunch of silver grass and pulled out an ordinary palm-sized rock. She placed the rock in Odo's hand, then blandly turned and walked out of the garden.

Overmastered and humiliated, Odo watched her go. The shadows and patches of nebula wash filled in the empty place.

"Odo," Kira attempted gently.

"Major . . . I'd like to be alone, if you don't mind."

He held the rock as if he didn't know whether to drop it or throw it or turn into it.

"All right," she sighed. "If you need me, I'll be in the shuttle, trying to contact Sisko." When he looked at her with that suspicious concern typical of him, she said, "Don't worry—when I was in the Resistance, I learned to camouflage subspace messages with quantum interference. I taught this method to Sisko. If anyone intercepts the signal, all they'll read is a slight elevation in background radiation."

He seemed eased by that, or at least so wrapped up in his own rite of passage that he was willing to trust her to know what she was doing and not draw attention to this crooked paradise he had discovered.

"Good luck," he said.

She watched as he contemplated his rock, and struggled with a dozen ways to tell him she wanted him to find the happiness that had been missing from his burdened, expressive eyes.

All she could think of was, "You too."

CHAPTER
13

"DAD!"

Best sound in the universe. Always had been, always would be.

Ben Sisko shoved his way past his own crewmates as they all piled out of the airlock. "Hey, there, Jake!"

He snatched his skinny son out of midair and hugged him hard.

"I was afraid you weren't coming back," Jake muttered, choked up.

Sisko coughed up the one thing all kids want to hear, the one thing no commander could promise with a whole heart. "I wasn't about to let that happen, was I?"

The white lie brought relief into Jake's big brown eyes as the teenager pulled back. "You sure you're all right?"

Julian Bashir nudged past them, offering Jake a pat on the shoulder. "Nothing a few days of light duty won't cure."

Sisko looked over his son's shoulder—used to be looking over his head—and saw that Bashir's promise was about to shatter.

Admiral Necheyev stood back from the episode, passively watching with that blond-on-blond colorless face and schoolmarm civility, implying with her presence that he wasn't facing a weekend of recovery.

The admiral was chafing to talk business—he couldn't imagine what business could involve the admiralty at this point. Maybe she just wanted a report.

She hadn't needed to come all the way into deep space to get a report. . . .

Everyone was waiting for him, all hovering about while he finished his moment with his son. They wanted to get on with whatever was about to happen.

He slapped Jake on the shoulder. "I'm fine, really. Now go on home. I'll see you later."

Smiling, Jake glanced at the admiral, then ambled off down the corridor.

Sisko felt like ducking back to that airlock before he was caught with unfinished homework.

All he could do was approach the pallid admiral and wait to be addressed.

"Well, Commander," she said, "it appears your mission was an even greater success than we hoped."

"So I'm told," he answered. "Has the delegation from the Founders arrived on the station yet?"

"They're already meeting with representatives from the Federation Council and a dozen other Alpha Quadrant systems. We're hoping to have a treaty signed within a matter of days. And we have you to thank for it."

She started down the hall, so he had no choice but to follow. He gestured Dax and the others to come with them.

"It's really Lieutenant Dax and Chief O'Brien who deserve most of the credit. If they hadn't convinced the Jem'Hadar to hand them over to the Founders, none of this would be happening."

Necheyev scooped up Dax and O'Brien in one studious but not particularly generous glance.

O'Brien quickly said, "We were lucky the Jem'Hadar turned us over to the Founders."

"We just had to convince them that we were serious about peace," Dax added.

Sisko glanced back at her. She was hiding something.

"Actually," O'Brien said when he saw the glance, "it didn't take much convincing."

They didn't want to talk, at least not in front of Necheyev. They had a story to tell, he could bet. Dax was giving him one of those non-looks.

"I suppose," he dodged, "the only question is whether we can trust them or not."

He didn't mean to sound so uneasy, but he was uneasy. This was exactly what he had hoped for.

Why, then, was his stomach in his throat? If the

Founders wanted peace, what was the excuse for the brutal tactics inflicted upon any ventures into the Gamma Quadrant up until this point?

Surely not defense. There hadn't been anything to defend against. Many a tyrant bargained for peace while preparing for war.

He found himself unkind toward this new development. He had more at stake than Necheyev or any of these bureaucrats who possessed high perches from which they laid down the law, but which they had not helped to build.

Only the threat of a harsh defense would bring the Founders to the negotiating table, and even then, could the agreement be trusted? The Romulans and Cardassians hadn't been interested in halting their brutish expansion until they realized they could lose everything in an all-out fight with the free systems of the Federation.

On the other hand, alien races could have alien motives. . . .

"It's a risk, I know," Necheyev went on. Evidently she was trying to read his face, then ignore what she saw. "But both the Federation Council and Starfleet Command believe it's one worth taking. By the way, Commander, one of the Founders asked to see you the moment you arrived on the station."

Suddenly feeling as if the corridor were getting narrower and narrower, Sisko looked at her. "Asked to see *me?*"

"If you're not too busy."

"Oh . . . I think I can spare a few minutes. . . ."

"I know we've had our differences, Ben, but I want you to know what a fine job I think you've—"

Sisko ground to a halt. A Jem'Hadar soldier was standing at guard down the corridor.

He fought the instinct to go for his phaser as Necheyev told him, "It's all right, Commander. The Founders have asked that the Jem'Hadar handle security for them during their visit."

"Is that so," Sisko bristled. Ordinarily that wouldn't have been an outlandish request, or even particularly notable. But it wasn't every day that a proven enemy of the Federation, destroyers of a starship, and open murderers were invited to stand at arms inside a Federation outpost.

This wasn't normal. It wasn't even abnormal. It was outlandish. What was going on here?

"If these talks were being held in the Gamma Quadrant," Necheyev presumed, "we'd want our security people along as well. Enjoy your meeting."

She didn't even stop walking. She left him standing there at the door, face-to-face with a Jem'Hadar excuse for a face.

The Jem'Hadar stepped aside—the first time one had ever done that to him.

He didn't like it. "Thank you," he said.

"You're welcome," the soldier responded.

So they had taught their dogs to sit up and bark on command.

No, this wasn't right at all.

Suddenly he wished Odo were here to keep an eye on all this. Odo could be standing right here pretending to be a piano, and none of these intruders would be the wiser.

Of course, it might look a little suspicious if Sisko came into the meeting carrying a piano.

With a stewing glance back at his crewmates, he went in alone.

"Commander Sisko," someone said, "come in."

He didn't recognize the man's voice. Most of it was buried under the swish of the door closing behind him.

But he did recognize the appearance.

Startled, he stepped toward the charming high-boned face and small painted eyes of a man he'd never met, but didn't trust any farther than he could throw the station.

The young man's china-doll face, egg-sized cheekbones, and twisted buns of black hair absolutely contradicted everything he knew about his race of people.

They were dangerous—that he knew.

"I've looked forward to meeting you. I am Borath."

He approached, but didn't extend a hand, perhaps because Sisko's posture didn't invite a handshake.

"You're one of the Founders?"

"That's correct," Borath said. "You seem surprised."

"Not really. Only I hadn't realized until now that I've already met one of your people."

"You're referring to Eris, of course. Yes, she's one of us. Though she couldn't very well admit it while you were pointing a phaser at her. I'm glad to see you're not holding one now."

What a joke. Sisko could no more hold these

people prisoner with a phaser than catch sunlight in a bottle.

"Do I need one?"

"Not at all . . . you seem skeptical."

"Can you blame me?"

"No," Borath allowed. "I realize you have no reason to trust the Dominion. But you must understand we were only trying to defend ourselves."

Sisko swallowed a bitter grunt. "From what?"

"We felt threatened by your incursions into the Gamma Quadrant."

"Threatened? Like when you ordered the Jem'Hadar to destroy the *Starship Odyssey?*"

Borath shrugged, his poise intact. He didn't display any of the reaction Sisko was fishing for. "That was regrettable."

He didn't regret it a bit.

Aggravated at the words without the feelings, Sisko felt his blood go to slow-boil. "And the massacre at New Bajor? That was regrettable as well?"

"Commander, you risked your life to bring us a message of peace and friendship. We chose to accept your offer. Would you rather we refused?"

Blistered, Sisko found himself forced to back off. He couldn't blow all this just for the satisfaction of taking down a set of creatures who'd embarrassed him once before.

"No," he said evenly, and gave Borath the point.

"Good." Borath offered him a smile. Poison smile. "Because, believe me, Commander, an alliance between the Dominion and the Federation will be beneficial to both our people."

He wasn't telling the whole truth and they both knew it. This offer of peace was being delivered wrapped around a big stick. The Founders had called the Federation's bluff, so why were they backing down? Certainly not timidity at the idea of bloodshed—they had the Jem'Hadar to shed it for them.

Sisko pressed his lips tight. No point responding. He'd just be handing Borath evidence for the prosecution after he knocked the sublime alien's pretty head off.

The sentiment of peace was beautiful, but there just wasn't substance behind those eyes.

He wanted to reach out into the station and grab Necheyev by the collar and drag her in here to look into Borath's noncommittal eyes, drench her with that underlying ridicule—

Was he imagining it? Was he just personally offended that he was the person to do the talking for the Gamma Quadrant?

Okay, so he was offended.

Borath gazed at him with that smug satisfaction. He couldn't buy it. He only saw the lie in his eyes. Was he the only one who could see it?

"Doctor—welcome back!"

"Thank you, Garak. It's good to be back. Business keeping you busy?"

Julian Bashir kept walking as the Cardassian tailor fell in beside him. The crossover bridge gave the two of them a vantage from which the crowd here and down on the Promenade could be seen.

Lots of people, everywhere. DS9 wasn't the same as when the *Defiant* had left.

"I've missed you, Doctor," Garak said, those bony brows making goggles around his eyes. His blue-gray face was animated today, maybe more than usual. "I admit I was very concerned for your safety. Lunch hasn't been the same without you."

Bashir understood that Garak was hunting for gossip, details he might be able to siphon back to the Cardassian high command, perhaps return himself to favor with them.

"That's very kind of you to say, Garak. Hopefully things can start getting back to normal around here."

Garak looked over the railing at the heavy crowd below. "Oh, I doubt that's going to happen, Doctor. I doubt that very much."

Bashir had heard for days now this sad nostalgic muttering from DS9's regular inhabitants that things were just too changed for them, likely too crowded. Those who had come this far out in space didn't do so to walk in the thick of any populace.

He'd heard a hundred reasons so far. One more couldn't hurt.

"And why is that?"

"There's an old saying on Cardassia," Garak said. "'Enemies make dangerous friends.' And I fear the Dominion is going to make a very dangerous friend indeed."

"I take it you're referring to the peace talks."

"Exactly. I'm afraid these treaty negotiations are a mistake we'll live to regret."

As they started down the stairs to the main level, Bashir avoided mentioning the *"if* we live" element of that sentiment. "Is that your opinion or the opinion of the Cardassian Central Command?"

"The former, I assure you. The Central Command is very much in favor of this treaty, which, as far as I'm concerned, only justifies my fears."

"Well, I hope you're worrying about nothing."

They were approaching the infirmary, which meant that Bashir was about to be sprung from having to console another of his friends or stationmates or space-sick total strangers, unless somebody was waiting inside that examining room with a headache too big to get through the exit.

When the door opened before he and Garak got to it, he thought his next headache might be coming out to meet him.

But it was T'Rul, coming out with a bandage on her hand.

"Subcommander T'Rul, have you been hurt?" he asked.

"I had a minor disagreement with some Starfleet Security officers. They refused to allow me to speak with the Federation's negotiating team."

She glared at Garak, but said nothing to him.

Bashir asked, "What did you want to talk to them about?"

Things had been so good since getting back from the other quadrant . . . there was talk of treaty, no one had broken any bones lately, he had a date for tonight . . . but T'Rul's bottled rage was scratching a hole in his lifeboat.

"I wanted to protest the exclusion of the Romulan Empire from treaty negotiations!"

"I wasn't aware that anyone had been excluded," Bashir sputtered.

"Every great power in the Alpha Quadrant has been invited to participate, except *us.*"

Astonished and trapped in this abrupt new whirl, Bashir searched Garak's face for denial from the Cardassian sector, but there wasn't any.

Fumbling to ease the moment until he could get answers, he gasped, "There must be some mistake!"

"The mistake," T'Rul blasted, "is thinking the Romulan Empire will stand by and allow such a betrayal to go unchallenged. Believe me, Doctor, if a treaty is signed without our approval, it will mean war!"

She spun and stalked away, every muscle crying like a harp string that she meant what she said and she was on her way to implement that promise, even if she had to personally cut a thousand throats in the night.

Beside him, Garak watched her go. "Still feel I'm worrying for nothing, Doctor?"

"Commander? May I see you a moment?"

"Yes, Doctor, you and everybody else."

Ben Sisko leaned back in his lounge and turned off the music he'd been expertly ignoring.

"Is my son sick?"

The question did its job. Bashir paused in the middle of a step, before coming too far into the living room. "No, sir," the mellow young man said, his expressive eyes patterned with trouble, "and I know you don't like to have your home disturbed by station business—"

Rearranging his shoulders, Sisko folded his hands over his chest, making it obvious that he was busy relaxing and he wanted to concentrate real hard on it. "No. I don't. So this must be a social call, right?"

"Mmm—no, sir. I'm sorry . . . but this *is* a tad bigger than station business."

Only then did Sisko notice that Bashir's hands were clenched, his golden complexion blanched. "All right, Doctor," he said in a different tone. "Go ahead and tell me what's wrong."

"I saw . . . I ran into . . . Would you mind if I sit down, sir?"

"No, of course not. Sit."

"Thank you . . . I ran into T'Rul on the Promenade. I was with Garak, and she looked at him with the most awful hatred—"

"So a Romulan and a Cardassian had a dispute, and this shook you up?"

Nipping the inside of his lip to keep down a venomous grin, Sisko wallowed briefly in the Cardassians and the Romulans disliking each other. It gave each of them somebody else to hate and distrust and took some of the pressure off the Federation. Of course, for the record, he wanted everybody to play nice in the sandbox.

"Oh, no, sir, but the reason for the argument . . . Commander, T'Rul insists that the Romulans have been deliberately left out of treaty negotiations with the Gamma Quadrant, on the request of the Founders. Can you imagine why?"

Sisko plowed forward half out of his chair. *"What?"*

Bashir's big eyes got bigger. "Oh, I'm so glad you don't know! Then it's a rumor, isn't it?"

"It had damned well better be!" Sisko found himself on his unsteady feet. "T'Rul said this?"

"Why, yes, sir," the doctor confirmed. "And she didn't seem to have the slightest doubt . . . but what really bothered me was Garak's reaction. He didn't seem to be surprised about it, and he didn't even try to deny it. I understand that he's only a storekeeper here, but you know how much he wants to be back in favor with the Cardassian command. . . . You don't suppose he'd be in on something that no one has bothered to tell you? I can't imagine T'Rul's gotten everything straight. . . ."

Rage boiling, Sisko scratched for ideas or answers, a course of action, refusing to plunge out and confront anyone on this before he thought it out. That was a good question, but even as Bashir's soft voice posed it, Sisko had most of the reasoning worked out.

The Romulans wouldn't—couldn't—let this go by. A vast galaxy alliance, except for their corner? They were paranoid anyway, always accusing others of trying to hem them in whenever anyone stood up against their corrosive expansion.

He didn't actually give a tinker's damn about their feelings, except that this would prevent a war with the Dominion by assuring one with the Romulans.

At once it struck him. Was this what Eris and the Founders were up to? What better way to weaken or destroy any resistance in the Alpha Quadrant than to let the powers that be rip each other apart first. A very old and effective trick.

"If this is true," he said, "then I wasn't told because somebody knew I wouldn't put up with that kind of sideswiping going on right under my nose."

Bashir seemed tired and panicked at the same time. "Are they trying to take you out of the loop? Sir, these negotiations were your idea! You risked your life—your command!"

"And certainly not to foment a war with the Romulans. Somebody must know that's what'll happen."

Enough thinking.

He spun for the door.

Bashir stood up. "Where are you going, sir?"

"To have a talk with 'somebody.'"

"Commander, Admiral Necheyev is here to see you."

Battling the urge to tell Dax, "Oh, joy," Sisko stiffened a little at the desk in his office, summoned his civility, and said, "Send her in."

There she was. The very symbol of galactic bureaucracy.

Sisko surveyed Necheyev as she came into his office, prim as a statue and twice as pale, and vowed to look up Starfleet records and see just what strife and contention this person had been through to merit an admiral's pip.

"You asked to see me, Commander?" she began.

He shoved aside the slightest of greetings or any segue, and asked, "I understand that the Romulans haven't been invited to the peace talks."

"That's correct."

"I was wondering what prompted that decision."

She moved toward the desk. "The Founders requested that they be excluded."

"Did they say why?"

"They felt the Romulans would be a disruptive influence."

He leaned forward. "More disruptive than the Cardassians?" he roiled.

"They seem to think so," she said. "Do you have a problem with this, Commander?"

Rising from his seat, he wondered if he was still in the room or if she was just talking to the empty chair. "Whether I have a problem with it isn't the point. It's the Romulans we have to worry about."

Not a hint of emotion pressed into that flat brow of hers. "Commander, if this treaty is signed, and I'm confident it will be, we'll never have to worry about the Romulans again."

"You're sure of that?"

"Quite sure. After all, what chance would they have against the combined power of our new alliance?"

"They wouldn't have much of a chance at all," Sisko said.

"I'm glad we agree." The admiral paused, then continued, a placating tone in her voice. "Believe me, Commander, the Federation carefully weighed all the options before entering into these peace talks."

"I realize that—" Sisko began.

"Then," the admiral said, "we have nothing further to discuss, do we?"

CHAPTER
14

"Computer, I want you to transmit a subspace signal using a narrow theta-band frequency shifted into a background radiation domain."

"Working," the tinny computer voice bubbled back at Kira as she sat sore and overmedicated at the comm panel in the shuttlecraft. "Low-frequency signals are virtually impossible to isolate from background radiation."

Kira frowned and muttered, "Unless you know what to look for, and Sisko will know. *If* he's out there."

"Unable to transmit signal due to external interference," the computer twittered politely.

Wishing that just once the damned thing would swear at her and call her names for asking these wacky things, Kira shifted in her seat and gave a second of brain time to that one big remaining mystery—how this planet could have warmth and growth without any visible power source.

No sun. It just couldn't be this way, no matter how much those ectomorphs wanted to bubble around their lake. There had to be some kind of technology heating this place and forcing photosynthesis without light. External interference . . .

"Switch to theta band B," she said.

"Switching. Unable to transmit signal due to external interference."

There it was again. "Okay," she said. "Switch to theta band C."

"Switching," it said. "Unable to transmit signal. External interference at all frequencies."

Kira grinned. The computer almost seemed annoyed at her requests. It was telling her not to bother trying again. What kind of programming let a computer anticipate what she was doing and tell her she was being an idiot? Hell, it could be useful all over the galaxy!

Anyway, there it was. She'd hit a firewall. The computer wasn't going to do this all the way through the alphabet and into Klingon letters.

Time for a whole different kind of search.

"Identify source of interference," she ordered.

"Scanning . . . interference generated by thermal radiation, unknown power source."

Thermal radiation was just heat. How could heat interfere with trying to send a signal? But it *could* explain why there was warmth and growth and photosynthesis on a planet with no sun.

Well, maybe not the photosynthesis, but one thing at a time.

Ignoring the shooting pain through her chest, she leaned forward abruptly. "Locate power source!"

"Power source is located three miles below the planet's surface, bearing one-two-seven, mark three."

"Can you identify?"

"Unable to identify due to presence of unknown poly-metallic substance within surrounding rock face."

She started to ask for a breakdown of that substance when Odo appeared at the shuttle entrance, and Kira clamped her mouth shut.

How much could she tell him without "also" telling those blobs out there? How much had they "merged" with him?

"Any luck, Major?" he asked.

Well, it *sounded* like Odo. . . .

She flipped a mental coin and came up on the talking side.

Okay—

"There's some kind of power source interfering with my signal. Any idea what it can be?"

He came all the way in, solemn and depressed as ever. No, in fact he was more depressed than ever.

"I haven't a clue," he muttered. He didn't seem to care, either, which wasn't like him at all.

She swiveled the chair around toward him. "Are you all right?"

He sighed. "I've just spent the last two hours shapeshifting. Rocks, flowers, trees . . . I've been everything in that garden."

"And?"

"And . . . nothing. Oh, I can *become* a rock all right," he said miserably, "but I have no more of an idea what it's like to *be* a rock than I did before."

The pointlessness of such petty fabrications shone in his voice and the slump of his long body on the seat.

She almost popped off something about who the hell wants to be a rock anyway, but decided better. "I'm not sure I know what that means," she dodged.

"I'm not sure either," he simply said. "And that's . . . unfortunate. Now, if you'll excuse me, I have to return to my bucket."

He unceremoniously plodded toward the aft of the shuttle, picked up his bucket and left the shuttle. Somewhere out there he would slurp into a cold pail while there was a whole lake of others out there, presumably of his own kind, swirling and whirling and cavorting in their own little paradise.

It wasn't fair.

Kira stared for a long time at the back of the shuttle, though all she could see was the bulkhead and the open passage.

Stupid shapeshifters.

Hadn't Odo displayed enough loyalty by coming back here? Finding them on a lost planet, out in the middle of an empty nebula? Why was it so much had to be proven?

Sick of proving herself all her life, if only to herself, Kira felt her chest swell with a heavy surge of empathy for Odo. How much did they expect of him?

Become a rock? Come on.

So he was a rock. So what? So he was a stick. So he was a mud pie.

What could all that mean? "How" to be a rock?

She was getting more and more sure just where the rocks were.

On a sharp decision, she got up and headed for the exit, without even telling the computer to keep working while she was gone.

"Hello? I need to talk to one of you."

Sparing a bruised thigh, Kira walked along the lakeshore, stopping, then walking, then stopping again. How exactly should a person talk to a giant blob of glue?

"Can anyone hear me?" she called, a little louder.

She almost jumped out of her skin when a column of mercurial gunk floated up out of the lake and drew together into a man's form with a face something like Odo's.

"We hear you, Major," he said. "But please be brief. We find the humanoid shape awkward."

Clearing her throat, Kira strode across the fresh grass, but didn't get too close. It was irritating how this creature snubbed the humanoid shape, even after they had condemned at least one, and maybe more, of their own kind to endure that shape which they found "awkward."

"I won't keep you long," she said. "It's about Odo. He needs your help."

"How would you have us help him?"

Wasn't this the concrete question of the month? Millions of space miles, a lifetime of searching, subliminal devotion to match any religion, and Odo was made to go sleep in a bucket?

She held back for a beat, then resolved to be civil.

"By sharing your knowledge with him." *You insensitive tub of latex—* "By talking to him. Telling him what he needs to know."

A few seconds flowed by, but all he said was "In time all his questions will be answered."

He's already put in the time, you glue guru.

She nodded impatiently. "And when will that be?"

"When he's ready to hear them."

Oh, this was just great. Perfect. Elastic non-answers. Odo could get this out of any summer poetry workshop.

"And you'll be the ones to decide that?" she presumed.

He moved a little. "Who better? After all, he's one of us. We know him."

"I 'know him' too."

The male shapeshifter was either bored or curious, but certainly dismissive. "Do you?"

"I'm his friend," she proclaimed in a tone that said she meant the whole phrase sincerely.

He stepped closer to her, but spoke with flat contempt. "You're a solid. All you have ever done is to teach him to be like you."

Irritable now, Kira refuted, "That's not true."

"Isn't it? If you really cared about your friend,

you'd stop interfering and let us do what's best for him." He paused, then tilted his chin downward slightly. It might have been candidness or condescension—she couldn't tell which. "It's time you went home, Major," he said. "Odo no longer requires your presence here."

So she was declared free to go by the reigning power.

Was she wrong? Were they pacing Odo in a way that was right for them? For him?

Why don't I have all the answers? Friends are supposed to have a few answers for each other.

She stood in silence and watched him slurp back into the lake, and wondered if she had said too much, and just how many beings she had just said it to.

Maybe I just got the answer.

"That's very good, Odo. Now, don't worry about holding your shape. You will. Just let go. Allow yourself to feel the texture of the stone . . . the warmth of the sun on the water. Allow it to become real to you."

The waters of a fountain shimmered in thousands of drops and sang a brittle song, imitating the efforts of a dampered harp. A chance for music, but difficult.

"Don't be afraid."

Droplets like bits of King Arthur's polished armor . . .

Odo heard the muffled voice of the female shapeshifter tinkling through his mind, for a moment blended with his own thoughts and only tacitly separate. The voice was a series of vibrations, a tickle across his surface. Were there insects? Or was she speaking again?

He rolled quickly downward, tumbling, rising, spraying, gathering into the pool of himself and going again. Leisurely, yes, unhurried and slapdash. Concentrate. Go and discover quintessence.

It just couldn't be done this way . . . the tedium erased any holiday emotions.

Part of him slipped away—just a few drops. Aware that he was being tested, he resisted the urge to reach out and catch them back. How could they take a piece of himself? Surely they would not keep the pieces. He was a singular being, separate unto himself, with identity and purpose.

He hungered for those droplets.

A sheet of water washed over his eyes, grew thinner and thinner, and was finally absorbed by his body.

And he could see her clearly now. The drizzle was gone.

There was something to be said for solid eyes.

"How do you feel?" the female asked him.

"Like a baby learning to walk," he said. When she tilted her head at him, he added, "It's a 'solids' expression."

She regarded him passively. "You *have* lived among them too long."

If the statement was meant to offend, it worked. "Why do you dislike humanoids so much?" he asked. "I know they have their flaws, but I've known many of them to be kind and decent people."

"Like Major Kira?"

"Yes. Like Major Kira."

"Then you've been more fortunate than most changelings."

The words drew him across that line of thought and into another. "Changelings?"

Had she expected him to react this way? Had she used the word on purpose?

She gazed at him, still reserved. "It's a name given to us by the solids. They meant it as an insult. In defiance we took it and made it our own."

As he tried to move forward toward her, he almost slipped off the rock he was sitting on. Thought he was still water—

"Go on, please," he said.

There was a breath on the word *please,* a tiny surge that betrayed his deep desire to know what he was and how it was more than just trickery. There had to be more.

More, more . . .

The female peered into his human eyes, eyes fabricated and fake—or had they become a clearer expression of himself over all these years than he ever would have admitted before this?

She saw something in them. The reaction was in her own superficial windows.

"The great link," she began slowly, "tells us that long ago our people used to roam the stars, searching out other races, so that we could add to our knowledge of the galaxy. We came in peace, but too often we were met with suspicion, hatred, and violence."

"Why?"

"The solids feared our metamorphic abilities. We were hunted, beaten, killed. Finally we made our way here. And here . . . safe in our isolation, we made our home."

"Tell me," he pursued, "why was I sent away?"

"Because even in our solitude we desired to learn more about the galaxy. You were one of a hundred 'infants' we sent off to gain that knowledge for us."

He searched for that ring of truth he had come to look for in his years of experience. She had entreated him in the way of her people—their people—to relegate suspicion to the past, even in the way she explained the past. Yes, he suspected her. He was an officer of the law more than he was anything else, and he wanted the hole filled.

These were convenient answers, these things she was telling him. Yes, some races of solids were violent and quick to react, but in all the galaxy there were pockets of wisdom. He knew. He had taken whiffs of those pockets, whether she believed him or not. To have isolated themselves as a nation, these shapeshifters had made a premature decision. Were they here to justify it to him and make him hide too?

He didn't want to hide. He wanted to grow.

"But how could you be sure we'd find our way here?"

"You had no choice," she said. "The urge to return home was implanted in your genetic makeup."

"You mean the need to learn about my past? It was all part of the plan?"

It seemed illogical to him, and he involuntarily frowned. To send messengers to learn about the outside, yet imprint them with an overwhelming desire to learn within—

"Yes," the female went on. "And now, thanks to the passageway, you are the first to return to us. We were not expecting you so soon."

Another clue. Another chance for a concrete answer. "When were you expecting me?"

"Not for another three hundred years."

He almost slid off the rock again as the revelation sliced into him. Three *hundred* years . . . Earth years?

How long had he been alive? Were there blocks of darkness in his mind for which he must also search?

Steeling himself, he pressed for the answers that might hurt.

"How long was I away?" he said on one breath.

"A long time," she responded. "But all that matters now is that you're back."

No, she wasn't going to give him that yet, he could see. She was falling back to the vague. Or possibly the language was failing her.

He sat back and sighed, not entirely hiding his disappointment. "It's different than I imagined it would be."

She saw his emotions, even in this imperfect, solid form he wore on the outside, a form that had become more comfortable than he had ever before realized.

To his utter surprise, she reached out and poured the droplets that had come from his liquid form back into his hand. The silver dots immediately blended with the human hand he held between them.

"Whatever you imagined," she said, "I promise the truth will be better."

Surprise took him again as she reached for him, but now her hands were not hands any longer. She was holding his hands now.

No . . . not hands either. Long liquid plumes of bright silver—he so seldom looked at himself when parts of him were changing—

Slowly he felt his torso being drawn toward her as well, and a movement set in where a moment ago there had been a shell of skin and an infrastructure of bone.

Yes, he had made bones for himself, even though it wasn't really necessary to the illusion of solidity. Why had he done that so long ago, and learned it so well?

His thigh quivered and dissolved into jelly. Hers were there too, liquid now.

Until only their heads remained in humanoid form, he felt himself blending with her, swelling with memories that weren't his, a blur of past and hope and fears.

So many fears, so many guesses . . .

Such beauty . . . such unblemished bursting passion . . .

Her face drew closer. His sight gave way to fluid silver, then blended through to something even more fundamental.

And the dark planet around them was only a pedestal.

And he was alien to himself.

CHAPTER
15

QUARK'S BAR. Noisier than usual, narrower than usual, today poisoned with the presence of dozens of Jem'Hadar who had discovered the Dabo table.

Julian Bashir resisted the sensation of claustrophobia. The bar was crowded today. Beside him, O'Brien was eyeing the crowd with the same tolerant disdain. Their home had changed.

Bashir looked at O'Brien and wondered if this could be the last straw for Miles and his wife. Keiko had not liked DS9 at first, and he wasn't sure she'd ever come to like it. The two had come off a starship, clean and fresh, manned with crew in bright, sharp uniforms, without a single bad element from which they had to protect their little daughter.

Regret piled into Bashir's chest at the thought of losing O'Brien. It hadn't been easy making friends here. They were all so busy, and so easily suspicious of each other—a band of misfits, each towing baggage of a painful past, none ready to trust.

What trust they had gleaned here had been at danger's point. Deep space, nine stations out.

And here they sat, in a pathetic mimicry of a pub, enduring the presence of rabble and quarrelers, larcenists and pirates, those who inevitably were pushed out onto any frontier by the expansion of decency as they ran before it in a shabby attempt to profit before it arrived.

Starfleet, Commander Sisko, the doctor and the engineer—*we're the ones with the badges on, supposed to tame the wild.*

It didn't look to Bashir as if it could be tamed.

"Excuse me, pardon me, after you, look out, coming through—"

That was Quark's voice. There was a drone about it, but also a particular ring of satisfaction as well.

"Sorry to keep you waiting, gentlemen," the Ferengi said as he appeared out of the crowd. "That's two synthales—on the house."

Both Bashir and O'Brien cranked up to stare at him.

"What's put you in such a good mood?" O'Brien asked.

"Isn't it obvious? Business is better than ever!" Quark deposited a bowl of salty nuts on the table and lowered his voice. "I admit I was a bit nervous at first, what with starships blowing up and rumors of invasions through the wormhole . . . but I have inside information that the peace agreement is about to be finalized."

Bashir cupped his hand around his drink. "And where did you get this information? From one of your 'friends' on the Federation Council?"

Quark stood back and puffed up. "If you must know, I overheard two Jem'Hadar officers talking—"

Bashir smiled, taking his moment's cheer in the fact that Quark could take such pride in his eavesdropping talent. "And you believed them?"

"I don't see why not. Oh, I know we got off to a rocky start, but they're not so bad, really." He gazed at the burly Jem'Hadar soldiers pounding about at the gambling table and approved. "I think they have the gene."

O'Brien glanced at Bashir, and when he got only a shrug from the doctor, he looked up at Quark again. "What gene?"

"The gambling gene. They've barely been at the station for a week and already they can't drag themselves away from the Dabo table."

Drowning his words in a sip, Bashir said, "How fortunate for you."

Beaming with success and no small measure of power, Quark placed a hand on each of their shoulders. "How fortunate for all of us. You see . . . I have a dream. A dream that one day all people—human, Jem'Hadar, Cardassian, Ferengi —will stand together in peace . . . around my Dabo table."

He gazed off into the surmountable future, seeing the twinkle of coins and the curl of bearer notes.

Bashir and O'Brien shared one of those glances they sort of hoped the subject would catch in his periphery. But Quark was involved in his mental ear-stroking and enjoying the rising noise from his gambling table.

Bashir leaned forward and glanced at O'Brien again. "You're a regular visionary, Quark."

The Ferengi sighed in his joy. "I am, aren't I?"

O'Brien leaned back to drain his glass. Bashir recognized the motion as an attempt to get out from under Quark's companionable grip and to keep his mouth shut on that one.

All of a sudden there was liquid streaming down O'Brien's uniform and he was coughing—he'd been hit from behind by a passing Jem'Hadar.

"You're in my way," the soldier barked down at O'Brien.

O'Brien glared up, but kept control. "Sorry."

He tucked his ribs to bring the chair closer to the table. The Jem'Hadar lashed out.

The engineer hit the floor in a heap, his beer landing on top of him, his face screwed up.

"Now, look here!" Bashir pushed forward and tried to get to O'Brien.

The Dublin express didn't wait. O'Brien burst to his feet and thundered past him. "Out of my way—"

Pillaging Quark's paradise in a single crash, engineer and alien pounded in a barrel roll across another table. Glasses and liquid pasted the patrons.

"Gentlemen!" Quark shouted. "Remember my dream!"

Bashir pushed through the loud harping crowd, struggling to get through the sea of shoulders and armor and body odor to where the Jem'Hadar and O'Brien were discussing their innermost philosophies. Crude punches and kicks served well enough, but he could see from here that O'Brien was flushed and overmatched. There was no blow that a bare human fist could land on a Jem'Hadar and have much more than a bruising effect. Their uniforms were armored and, beneath those, their bodies were also armored. These were upright iguanas, blessed by evolution with something close to an outer skeleton.

Only such beings could afford to be so easily enraged.

He saw the Jem'Hadar's eyes, white-ringed and blazing, for he was chewing O'Brien's guts in his mind.

More and more the battle tilted toward the decidedly one-sided. Bashir pushed and squeezed, but he could barely make any headway against the cheering, betting crowd that didn't care who won as long as the floor got bloody.

"That's enough!" he shouted. He tried to reach past the Jem'Hadar, who had O'Brien on the ground now and was crushing the life out of him. "That's—"

The soldier turned on him, and caught Bashir's throat in one of those ten-pound claws they called hands.

Bashir hammered at the Jem'Hadar's arm, but the grip was like granite. He clutched the Jem'Hadar's wrist, catching in his periphery a glimpse of O'Brien lying on the floor, hacking and pulpy, sucking air and wincing.

The periphery began to close. Bashir tried to draw a breath, but the hand around his throat was closing in. His hands trembled as strength fell out of his arms. He couldn't fight and no one was helping him. Would they stand by and let him be killed?

"All right! What's going on here!"

Security officers piled into the ring. The grip suddenly fell away from Bashir's throat. He dropped back, pulled a huge gasp, then used the crowd around him to claw his way to O'Brien.

Security Chief Eddington and at least one other Starfleet Security guard were slamming the Jem'Hadar back against a replicator.

"What's going on?" Eddington demanded again.

The Jem'Hadar pointed at O'Brien. "He addressed me in a disrespectful manner."

Bashir looked up from trying to straighten O'Brien so the poor man could breathe. "That's a lie."

"Easy, Doctor," Eddington said. "We're all friends here."

"Tell *him* that."

Eddington pressed up to the Jem'Hadar offender and said, "I'll see this doesn't happen again."

The Jem'Hadar leered into his eyes. "I expect you will."

And the former enemy turned and strode freely out of the bar.

"That's it?" Bashir derided to Eddington. "You're just going to let him walk away?"

"Our orders are to give them a wide berth."

"I know what the orders are! But he attacked

Chief O'Brien. We have rules here against that sort of thing!"

"I'm aware of station regulations, Doctor," the young man said. "However, the Jem'Hadar are not. We have to allow them some time to get used to our customs."

Bashir gaped up at him, clearly outraged. "And in the meantime, they're free to do whatever they want?"

Eddington discarded him with a blink. "Remember that before you get into another brawl with them."

He nodded to the other Security man and together they picked their way over collapsed tables and overturned chairs and left the bar much the same as they'd found it. No warnings, no citations, no questioning, no simple justice.

O'Brien moaned. Bashir pulled his attention from incredulous fury to bedside manner.

"You'll be all right, Miles," he said, mostly just to hear his own voice and cling to it. The engineer's body was hot, flushed, all muscles tensed with pain. "Don't move. You've a broken rib or two, I think . . . no, no! Stop—he's gone. Don't fight."

"Where's the—dirty bastard?" O'Brien coughed and tried to sit up.

Pressing his hands to O'Brien's arm and side, Bashir tried to keep him down, but when that failed he slipped a hand behind the chief and helped him keep upright enough to breathe better. "He's gone. It's all over. Someone give me a glass of water!"

"Water?" Quark responded from somewhere behind the onlookers. "I don't serve water!"

"All right," Bashir said. "At least someone call a medical team. Have them bring an antigrav gurney and a first-aid kit."

Beneath his hands, O'Brien struggled again. "Julian . . . did they arrest him?"

"No . . . no, they didn't." He lowered his volume. "Please stop moving, for God's sake, before you crack in half. He wasn't pulling his punches. He was out to kill you."

"That was assault—" O'Brien choked. "He hit me. . . ."

"Miles, shut up, please." Bashir glanced around the bar. Yes, there were still other Jem'Hadar hovering in the background, ready to be incited.

He didn't have to ask again. O'Brien curled in pain and was lost to his own wounds. Lying here unprotected, without a friend in the crowd who would put his neck on the line by lending a hand, Bashir and his patient waited for medical help.

It was obvious now that they weren't going to get any other kind on *Deep Space Nine* anymore.

Ben Sisko played with his food like a two-year-old. For a long time now—he had no idea how long—he had chased one bean around his plate, ignoring the heaps of dumplings and vegetables. He was going to get that bean, but it had to be arranged just right on the fork. It was the last one and he wanted it to do what he told it to do. He wanted authority over that bean.

"Dad?"

The bean bumped up against a crushed dumpling.

When had the dumpling been forked? He didn't remember doing that. It looked cold. The gravy was getting a skin.

"Dad, pass me the potatoes."

He wanted to get the bean away from the dumpling without getting gravy on it. He touched it with the tine of his fork to see how stuck it was.

"Dad?"

Sisko's dream about the bean cracked and he looked up. "Yes, Jake—what is it?"

His son regarded him from across the table as though surveying an escaped lunatic. "The potatoes?"

"Oh . . ."

"Dad, is something wrong?"

Sisko tried to shrug, but didn't get it out. "Not really. I'm just a little preoccupied, that's all. It's these Dominion negotiations."

"What about them?"

A year ago Sisko would never have considered discussing something like this with his son. Today, though, and ever since he'd returned from the Gamma Quadrant, he'd found his son to be the only person he could speak to, the only one who wouldn't get in trouble for talking to him, wouldn't be watched by eyes around the corners. And he hadn't told Jake much. He was afraid to.

Everyone knew he was against what was happening, so no one who didn't trust him would speak to him, and he didn't want to foist the authorities on anyone who did trust him. Jake was the only person that Starfleet wouldn't consider questioning.

How long would that remain?

His son was tall now, tall enough to be thought of as an adult. *How much longer can I protect him?*

"It's all happening behind closed doors," he said. "I guess I feel like I've been cut out of the loop."

Jake nodded, but didn't turn back to his food. "No," he said, "it's more than that. There's something going on, isn't there?"

Sisko smashed the bean with his fork and scooped it up. "Like what?"

Jake wasn't so easily put off anymore. "You tell me."

There. His son knew this wasn't a joke or a game. Sisko felt transparent.

The door chime saved him from explaining to Jake the squandered possibilities of this great galaxy, the crumbling ladders so lately forged into the darkness by the Federation. Suddenly sad that he wouldn't have a chance to vent his plagued thoughts, Sisko put his fork down. "Come in."

But Jadzia Dax was already halfway across the room.

"Benjamin, did you know about this?"

As agitated as he had ever seen her, she wagged a padd before him.

"Know about what?" he asked.

"I've been transferred to the *Lexington*. I'm its new science officer!"

He thrust himself to his feet. The napkin slipped from his thighs to the floor. "There must be some mistake!"

She shook the padd again. "I have the orders right here." Her porcelain complexion was flushed and she was holding back from pacing.

He snatched the padd. "Let me see that. I don't believe it—"

"Bashir to Sisko."

Damn it—he should have that blasted comm unit blasted.

"Go ahead, Doctor."

"Commander, I need to talk to you about the Jem'Hadar."

He looked at Dax, and together they wondered what else could go wrong.

"Come with me," he said.

"What happened?"

Sisko piled into the infirmary and almost skidded into the table with O'Brien stretched out upon it, beaten so much he looked like those dumplings back on that plate. Keiko was in the background, drinking a cup of coffee. She nodded to him, but didn't say anything.

And she had that look on her face that Sisko had been seeing so much lately—that look of fatigued disdain, as if she didn't know what to do to keep going, as if the simplest answers of daily life were suddenly elusive.

He didn't enjoy that expression. In fact, he was plain sick of it. How could the same expression get on so many faces of so many races?

"Chief?" He looked down at O'Brien. Conscious, at least. "Who did this?"

"Jem . . . Jem . . ."

"A Jem'Hadar soldier we bumped in Quark's," Bashir filled in. "Literally bumped, sir . . . Miles just leaned back to swallow his drink, and this fellow shoved him right off his chair. After that, why, it was a free-for-all. It's never been like that before in Quark's. Crowded and rowdy and—"

"And they let him go!" O'Brien declared, trying to raise his head.

"Yes!" Bashir confirmed. "That Eddington character didn't even press charges! I couldn't believe it." He touched O'Brien's arm in a gesture of support and added, "This wasn't just a barroom brawl. That beast was out to kill him."

"Did anyone try to talk to Eddington?" Sisko asked.

"Commander?" Keiko O'Brien joined them, drawn by her husband's pathetic efforts. "I tried to talk to him, but I was told that Security just wants to keep the trouble down, no matter what happens. He refused to prosecute any Jem'Hadar. He said it just like that! Sir, are we going to have to live like this?"

Sisko started to answer her, the rote answers that piled up against the back of his teeth, things he'd learned to say since becoming a station administrator that would quell problems and reset values.

But his own rage piled up too. He didn't want to quell this. He wanted the vibrations of tumult to rise here. Let all the people about him foment what he saw in Keiko's face, in Bashir's, in O'Brien's. If DS9 had to be the hingepin of rebellion, so be it.

No. They couldn't live like this.

He didn't even see the corridors as he charged through them. Didn't notice the door open when he stormed into the wardroom. He hesitated as he absorbed the room, then veered to the table where

Admiral Necheyev and Borath were poring over some star charts as casually as if they were doing a jigsaw puzzle. Maybe that's what they really were doing. Parceling out civilization.

"I want to know what the hell is going on," he demanded.

Necheyev's pinched face rose before him. Oh, if only she weren't a woman—

Necheyev squared her thin shoulders. "Commander, I don't appreciate your barging in here."

"I want to know why my science officer's been transferred without my consent. I want to know why my chief of operations is lying in the infirmary, while the Jem'Hadar soldier who brutally beat him is free to walk the station. And I want to know why the Federation is willing to risk a war with the Romulans to form an alliance with a group of people we hardly know and barely trust."

Her little nose went up. "Are you finished?"

"I haven't even begun."

"Admiral," Borath said, "I think you should tell Commander Sisko what he wants to know."

Catching implications in the sentence, Sisko backed off a step and demanded with his demeanor that they follow through on that, and go past it to the completeness of their plans. He *was* going to understand this.

Necheyev was resisting. She didn't want to give in. She liked playing her games of closed doors and galactic chess.

He fixed his glare on her. If he had to, he would resort to just being bigger, meaner, and definitely madder.

"All right," she said. "I suppose he deserves to be the first to hear the news."

Was he supposed to thank her?

"What news?" he asked.

She started pacing, that nasty, pompous little stroll she did when she thought she had the upper hand.

"The Federation is pulling out of this sector. All Starfleet personnel currently stationed on DS9 will be reassigned to other posts. Yourself included."

Sisko felt his arms melt at his sides, his stomach kick upward until his throat knotted. Her spiritless announcement gnawed at him as he gathered instantly all the implications, the broken promises, the petty handoffs.

He openly scorned her. "What about Bajor's entry into the Federation!"

"Those plans are on hold for the time being." Necheyev's chin bobbed downward and her head tilted to one side, her eyes batting upward, as if she were tolerating him out of her own generosity. "From here on, Bajor will be the Dominion's responsibility. They'll be running the station."

"Are you telling me the Bajorans have agreed to this?" he blazed at her.

"We're confident they'll have no objection."

In other words, nobody had the guts or the decency to mention it to the people whose destinies were closest to this monumental gaffe. Sisko snapped back, "And if they do object, what then? You send in the Jem'Hadar?"

From the other side of the table, Borath spoke to

him with the same condescension. "The Jem'Hadar are used only against our enemies. Bajor will be protected, Commander. We'll see to it."

Sisko ignored him and continued to face down Necheyev. "What about the wormhole? Do they get to protect that too?"

"It's the price of peace, Benjamin."

"Well, if you ask me, the price is too damned high. What's the Federation supposed to get out of all this?"

"Our friendship," Borath replied. "Isn't that enough?"

"And you, Benjamin," Necheyev added, "get a promotion. Captain Sisko. That's an important step toward that admiralcy you've always wanted."

So they wanted to buy him off, shut up the person who knew this area best, and best understood the implications of dealing with the Dominion. *Why? What the hell is going on?*

What powers were coming into control at the Federation Council? He knew those people—they weren't like this. They couldn't possibly understand what they were about to do, or they wouldn't do it.

"Admiral, I'd like a chance to speak to the Federation negotiating team before this treaty is signed," he declared, forcing himself to breathe evenly and at least put up a front of reason. He knew he wasn't going to get anywhere with these two. He couldn't even break anything under these conditions.

Necheyev was as immutable as granite as she stood before him. She gave him his answer with her eyes even before she spoke.

"It's too late for that, Ben. The treaty was signed late this afternoon."

Sisko stared at her. In his mind he saw the station and the wormhole and the planet of innocent Bajorans and all the future built here whirling down into a single pit of complete betrayal.

Borath moved to Necheyev's side. "It's the beginning of a new era. And you helped make it possible. Congratulations."

CHAPTER
16

"ODO? ARE YOU HERE?"

The grasses and vines whispered in the ornamental garden. The fountain chittered nearby.

Kira's conversation with the shapeshifter clung to her like guilt as she wandered through the garden, up to and past the place where she had sat with Odo and listened as well as she could to what his rite of passage was doing to him.

She faced a big catalpa bush on its way to being a tree if somebody didn't trim it.

"Odo?" she tried again. "I'm going to try to track down the source of the interference blocking my theta-band signal. If I can't find it and neutralize it, I guess I'll have no choice but to leave here and try to find Sisko and the others." A faint smile pulled at her lips and she tried to let part of it out without losing too much control. "I'm glad you finally made it home, Odo . . . I know things are going to work out for you and—"

The tree shivered as a long branch from some other bush brushed against it. Maybe it was a breeze, maybe just a vibration—she wasn't sure.

"I don't believe this," she mumbled. "I'm talking to a tree. You're probably not even here, are you?"

There went dignity for the "solids" if any of those other beach balls were watching from the wings.

She clamped her mouth shut. She'd been entertaining enough.

With as much military elegance as she could muster, she solidified her way back to the shuttle, assuming she was being watched all the way.

Why hadn't she thought of that? They weren't just the lake. They could be anything around her, listening and snickering. That's probably what that bush was doing when it rustled.

There was more of a mystery here than how small a mouse those beings could morph themselves into. There was a power source here and she meant to find it.

The shuttle was in good working condition. Computer-generated repairs had been made on a few systems that had suffered during the attack on the *Defiant*. It was warm and quiet on board.

"Computer," Kira began, "can you pinpoint that power source previously reported?"

"Affirmative."

"Is there a source of breathable atmosphere down there also?"

"Affirmative."

"Describe the terrain there."

"Solid rock consisting of limestone and shale, with considerable cavern area—"

"That's good enough for me. Find me a rock I can stand on. Transporter . . . energize."

It was a cavern, all right. Not particularly pretty, as caverns went. And there was a light source somewhere too. Dim, but here somewhere, casting shapes on the rocks where there was no protrusion.

Why would there be light down here and not on the surface?

Fabricated power source, obviously, not natural. No matter how fluid and lovely those shapeshifters appeared or how simply they dressed, they were technologically based or harboring somebody who was.

Good. Kira liked simple answers, and right now she was on a hunt to add to her collection.

Caverns . . . atmosphere . . . for a gaggle of beings who didn't need either.

Or did they? Could shapeshifters do without air?

She scraped through her memory to see if Odo had gone somewhere without oxygen, without gravity—just what were the limits of their abilities? Did they have abilities Odo didn't know about yet? Were they more practiced at being what they were than he was? Did they have tricks he didn't know about?

Friends—in spirit, perhaps, she and Odo, yes. But had they ever shared these things with each other? Had she cared enough to ask him about his past and how he came to know of himself as a shapeshifter? How many years it took him to cull out the legends from the facts . . . how much pain and fear had been thrown in his face before he found his way to DS9, where he had purpose and responsibility and deeply cherished both. No, she'd never asked the way friends ask—just for the sake of knowing.

A glint of metal caught her attention. Metal or just a deposit of shale or mica?

She moved toward it, cautious of chipped stones beneath her feet and gaping holes that she might not see until it was too late. Metal, definitely. Rather a large—

A door?

Embedded in the rock face was a sizable panel of manufactured metal, with a separation between the metal and its rock face enough to slip a knife into. This wasn't any accident or remnant of a wreck. This thing was built this way.

Obvious conclusion number one. Moving along . . .

"Why would shapeshifters need a door?" she murmured aloud.

Oh, the sound of her own voice was reassuring as it tumbled through the cavern.

Her tricorder burped and coughed when she tried to scan for a reading. It provided her with the construction of the door, but not what was beyond it.

She tapped her comm badge.

"Kira to shuttle computer. Scan the area one hundred and eighty meters dead ahead."

"Scan unable to penetrate interference," the computer returned without even the satisfaction of a pause for a moment of hope.

She let the tricorder fall to its strap, and stood before the door with her hands on her hips. In, she wanted *in*. There was always something behind a door and she wanted in.

She could take the risk of beaming directly in, but without a way to scan, she might be beaming into an open pit, or a chemical pond, or any description of quick ends. There had to be another way.

She turned her portable lamp on the edges. All the way up one side, around the top, down the other side—

A locking mechanism. Why hadn't her tricorder picked that up?

It was definitely there, though, not just wishful thinking. She stooped for a better look.

Out of reach, that's how it looked. This was a technical age, but that lock was basic and mechanical. It might be a backup; power had a way of shutting down. Sometimes locks still had a good old-fashioned key.

Well, that didn't help.

What would?

"Not what," she murmured aloud again. *"Who."*

Ornamental grasses and the fountain whistled and played around her. The starlit night and arms of nebula embraced the spraying waters. Crickets and birds that couldn't possibly be surviving here gamboled in their happy freedom.

She was getting sick to hell of it.

The bench under her was cutting into her thighs. Sooner or later, one of these blobs would come and talk to her. At least ask her why she hadn't gotten out of here yet.

Overhead, a large bird circled against the sparkling sky.

A bird? Animal life?

It came down more and more, landed in a tree near her, prattled down through a branch and into the bush beside her. She was about to get up, to put some distance between herself and the huge predator, when its body distorted and expanded, then drew together into a form she recognized.

Odo smiled as he came to sit beside her on the bench.

He was *smiling!* He didn't do that very often.

Pondering the fact that he could somehow make a bird's beak but not a person's nose—of course, maybe a bird wouldn't think it was so good—Kira shoved that aside and said, "Odo, I've been waiting for you."

"Major, I've just had the most remarkable experience," he said, beaming. "For a few short moments, I actually felt what it was like to be an Arbazan vulture. The air currents beneath my wings, the exhilaration of soaring above the treetops . . . it was all very stimulating."

"I'm happy for you." She was forcing her own

smile, but the words were easier than she expected, preoccupied as she was.

He looked at her. Warmly he said, "I know you are."

"So," she pushed on, "I guess you'll be staying here awhile?"

He gazed at her.

More gratitude rose in his eyes. Their years together, functioning and fighting side by side, suddenly truncated into not enough time.

"I've enjoyed working with you, Major," he said solemnly.

She nodded. "I've enjoyed working with you, too. . . . But before we say good-bye, I'm going to need your help one last time."

That seemed to please him. "Of course."

"Remember that power source I was telling you about?"

"The one preventing you from trying to contact Commander Sisko."

"Well, I've discovered its location, but I need you to help me examine it."

"What can I do?"

Relieved that in this one last way he was still with her, she adjusted herself on the bench. "There's a door blocking my path. I need you to help me get it open."

Odo frowned. "What kind of a door?"

"It's composed of some kind of metal the tricorder can't identify. But other than that, it's an ordinary door. The kind used by humanoids to get from one place to another."

Puzzled, Odo said, "That's odd. My people have no need for doors. They dislike taking humanoid form."

"I know."

"Then who could be using it?"

"Commander Sisko, does the Federation really expect Bajor to hand over *Deep Space Nine?* To hand over control of the wormhole? To hand all that we have over to the Dominion?"

Not a bad bunch of questions. Absolutely rhetorical. Nobody expected that of Bajor, at least not passively. Bajor's control over the wormhole was the only advantage this poor, underdeveloped, ravaged, and tired planet had in its favor. They'd come reluctantly into the Federation, distrustful of others, frightened of a Cardassian reorganization and new assault, willing finally to trust the Federation to help them help themselves. It had been an act of benign desperation, this trust, and the Federation had something to live up to.

Those words they had ridden in upon, that silver horse that, until now, had never stumbled.

Sisko gripped the edge of his desk and looked into the monitor, seeing the pale shock on Bajoran Minister Jod's face. Could Jod see the nausea on his? He hoped so.

He didn't know this man well, but he didn't have to.

"That's exactly what they expect," he admitted. It almost sounded like a desperate warning. Get out while you can—but there was nowhere to run.

"And I don't understand or agree with their reasoning any more than you do."

"Then why don't you try to talk some sense into the Federation Council?"

"I've tried. Their response was that I should follow orders and begin the evacuation of Starfleet personnel from the station."

Jod sat back, drained. "So that's it, then. The Federation has turned its back on Bajor."

The words trumpeted through Sisko's head. How often had Kira accused them of this and Sisko had to argue it down? Promise otherwise, swear otherwise? Now what was she going to say?

"Well, I have news for you, Commander," Jod swore. "Bajor has fought for its freedom before and if necessary we'll fight for it again. And if that means going to war with the Jem'Hadar, then that's what we'll do."

Sisko almost nodded, but kept from doing it. "I admire your courage, Minister Jod, but do you really believe Bajor could win such a war?"

"Alone? No. But we won't be alone." Jod pulled forward in his chair again, his chin stiff and his resolve screwed up tight. "The Romulans will be fighting alongside us."

"The Romulans?"

"They're as anxious to keep the Dominion out of the Alpha Quadrant as we are. So as of this morning, we've signed a pact pledging to stand together against the Jem'Hadar . . . and their allies."

Bajor as an enemy of the Federation, after all

this. Sisko gathered the picture in his mind. "I hope it doesn't come to that," he murmured.

Jod's lower lip bunched up as anger welled over the monitor and flowed into the office. "Then you'd better hope the Jem'Hadar stay on their side of the wormhole."

The transmission ended. Sisko could've sworn he heard a *crack* when Jod cut off the signal.

When had things gone out of control? A few weeks ago, there was a thriving station, a recuperating planet, a bright bridge to another place—now there was only this. Collapse. Abuse. Maybe war.

Definitely war. Definitely. Now that the Romulans had an ally, they would not remain still under Dominion incursion. They wouldn't wait for a war to gurgle out of skirmishes and incursions. They'd start one.

I don't blame them, Sisko thought. Empathizing with the Romulans?

Why not? Right was right and wrong was wrong, even in deep space. And this . . .

He walked the station. The whole station, from the docking pylons to the Promenade. No one spoke to him and he returned the favor. The faces of the hundreds of innocents, Bajorans, humans, even the Jem'Hadar soldiers who kept clear of him—probably under orders or temptations. They would have this whole station in a matter of days. They were holding their tempers until then.

When he had first come here, how he'd hated this place. How ugly and vulgar it had seemed to him.

It had been as far out into space as he could go and still manage to provide a semblance of civilization for his boy. As far away as he could get from wars and the Borg and the sour taste of his own rank and the death of his wife. He had nothing but bitterness to wear on his shoulder in those first weeks, and only the nagging hand of common sense kept him from surrendering his commission and living in a hut somewhere.

The station didn't look so vulgar to him today. He had learned to see the possibilities in the ugly Cardassian design and the clutter of beings who came here to hang out and escape from their own horrors. Or perhaps create a few.

The ten thousand headaches for him to deal with in the running of a critical outpost—those were the horrors. At the moment they weren't so horrible. Those endless nettles had walked him through losing his wife by making him think of what she would tell him if she were here, through raising his son by welding him in place and making him face up to it.

Ten thousand headaches had rebuilt his life. In the process, the lives of thousands of others had been undergirded. The whole planet below, Bajor, planet of rebels, planet of liberated captives, planet of refugees, finally had become a planet of free citizens constructing a future, leaning just enough on the broad shoulder of the Federation. Soon they would have pushed off, and been a bright star in someone's night sky.

Mostly mine. I never realized how proud of them I was. Kira never realized it . . . and I never knew to tell her. I was always telling her, "I assure you, I assure you." Why didn't I come right out and say, "I like the Bajorans, I'm proud of Bajor, and I'm going to defend all of you with my life"—

And it had come to this. Bajor talking about alliance with the Romulans. Certainly the Bajorans understood that alliance with the Romulans meant eventual dominance by them. They'd slipped into the one-step-at-a-time mode. How could the Federation fight against the Bajorans, who only wanted the freedom the Federation had promised them? He felt like a liar. He had so ferociously demanded that the Bajorans see the difference between the Federation and the tribalistic thugs that roamed this part of the galaxy. Benjamin Sisko would go down in Bajoran lore like the names of Judas or Benedict Arnold.

"Ah, Commander!"

Sisko blinked and winced. That was Garak's voice. He didn't turn to meet it. He didn't want to do station's internal business right now, squabbling with store owners who might or might not be spies. This just wasn't the moment.

He found himself sitting in the Replimat with his hand cupped around a cold mug of raktajino. When had he gotten here?

Fine. He was here.

"I was hoping to see you before you left," Garak said as he plunked into the chair beside Sisko. "I've wanted to tell you how impressed I've been by you the last two years. You run this station with strength, dignity, and compassion. Well done."

Sisko almost spat in his face.

Then he looked up and saw something he wasn't

used to in Garak's expression, something that wasn't usually there.

Honesty.

"Thank you, Mr. Garak," he forced out. "Your being here helped make those two years . . ."

"Interesting?"

A smile creased his cheeks and almost cracked his face. "Very interesting," he agreed.

Garak nodded. "I tried. . . . Oh, I'm sure you'll be back before long. Though from what I've heard, when you return it'll be to fight against Bajor."

"I've heard the same rumors." Bile rose again. Sisko smoldered, "That Bajor has made a pact with the Romulans to make a stand against the Jem'Hadar . . . and their allies."

"The Bajorans have fought for their freedom before. It makes sense that they would fight for it again."

"So much for the results of my 'peace' mission."

"Do I detect a note of bitterness in your voice?"

"I wouldn't be surprised."

"If it makes you feel better, I happen to share your feelings about the Dominion treaty." Garak bobbed his—well, eyebrows, if that's what those were. "I've given it a great deal of thought, and the only explanation I can find is that our leaders have simply gone insane."

He offered a strange little smile.

Sisko looked at him, then couldn't help but smile back. "It seems that way."

"Unfortunately," Garak went on, "there's nothing you or I can do about it."

"I suppose not."

"After all, you have your orders, and as for me . . . I would never dream of opposing the wishes of the Central Command. A pity."

Garak was looking at him. Fishing.

"I agree," Sisko said, heavy with implication. "That it's a pity."

"I thought you would."

More than anything, the Cardassian was proving how far down the barriers had been whittled on DS9, that perhaps the past two years had not been a vain dilation of somebody else's schematic.

"Mr. Garak," Sisko said, "I never knew we thought so much alike."

"Life is full of surprises, Commander."

"Commander Sisko!"

The shriek trumpeted down the open corridor, burying the conversation they were having. The crowd scrambled for cover—someone choked out a short scream. The first disruption Sisko saw as he vaulted to his feet were three Jem'Hadar soldiers plowing the citizens down.

Then he saw T'Rul, running at full tilt—

"There she is!" The Jem'Hadar had their weapons drawn.

Sisko raised his hand defensively, ready to shout that those weapons had better disappear, they were not allowed on the open Promenade, but two of the Jem'Hadar were already aiming.

"No!" Sisko blasted.

Two harsh streaks of energy bolted from the Jem'Hadar and both hit T'Rul square in the spine.

Momentum brought her crashing forward into Sisko. He caught her as she slipped to the deck, the fabric of her uniform and the skin beneath it curling, melted and trailing a thin finger of smoke.

Lashed to a fury, Sisko let the dead girl roll off his knee just as the three Jem'Hadar charged into the Replimat. He burst upward, took hold of one of their power rifles, then fell hard to one side and delivered the rifle butt into the gut of one of the soldiers, right into the solar plexus, if this animal had one.

Without waiting to see, he pivoted and smashed another Jem'Hadar full in the face with the rifle barrel.

But there were three Jem'Hadar, not just two, and he was out of moves and trying to regain balance too fast.

He bumped up against a thick armor plate and heard the heart beating behind it—or was this his own heart? There were voices and astonished faces around him, spinning and rising. Garak was calling his name.

He had never wanted to answer before, but today . . .

His throat burned. Air was sucked in, shoved out. And the Jem'Hadar were above him now.

And he couldn't see clearly anymore.

The Promenade was more crowded but less sociable than usual. Sociability had been on a downward spiral for days now. People walked, yes, but in a hurried manner, as though escaping from whoever was walking behind. Peace had been mutilated by treaty. The future was haywire in the face of shifting priorities.

No one knew who would be sacrificed next, which deck or which continent would be razed in the name of expansion. The humans and Klingons walked here in a rush to pack up. The Bajorans walked here as if covered with boils. Parents pulled their children through on the double. There was purpose in every step, subtraction in every glance. No one talked anymore.

People were leaving. Civilians, traders, any Federation national, all Starfleet personnel. Leaving this outpost they had hammered into salience without subsidy.

Now they must evacuate.

Julian Bashir had come to hate walking on the Promenade. Or anywhere else, for that matter. To walk anyplace other than the Promenade was to be met with flagrant suspicion from the guards posted where once there had been none.

Astounding—he had come to notice that this rough station, until recently, had required almost no formal policing actions. Sisko had demanded order, Odo had provided it. There had never been guards standing posts before.

Now they were everywhere. Protecting what? The visitors from the residents, or the other way around? No one was sure.

He stood outside the infirmary, watching, convincing himself of what he already knew.

Ah—friendly faces. Well, one friendly face and a facsimile. Dax and Garak.

"How's Chief O'Brien?" Dax asked.

"Still a little sore," the doctor answered, "but he should be in position by now."

Garak gestured down the corridor. "In that case, Doctor, I suggest we be on our way."

"Agreed," Dax said. "Let's go."

Bashir let his knuckles fall against the infirmary door as he dropped his hands to his sides. The door was cool and stable.

He would remember that.

Together they walked to the office of the chief of security and went in without announcement. Over Garak's shoulder Bashir could see Commander Sisko sitting in one of the holding cells.

Sisko was sitting with his elbows on his knees and his hands clasped. Even here, he was somehow part of DS9 or it part of him. Bashir resisted the urge to wave hello.

"Can I help you?" Chief Eddington looked up from his desk.

Dax swayed toward him. "We're here to see Commander Sisko."

"Sorry. My orders are that no one sees him."

Bashir tried to seem submissive. "But we're here on urgent business."

Eddington might have shrugged, or that might have only been a shift of his shoulders. "You'll have to talk to Admiral Necheyev. She's in charge here until the Jem'Had—"

Garak reached across the desk and shoved a Cardassian hypospray against Eddington's arm. Eddington slumped onto the desk and Bashir stared at him, wondering if the poor man was still alive—he was still breathing, yes.

"I'm sorry," Garak said flatly, "but we are rushed for time and I knew neither of you would feel comfortable striking a fellow officer."

While Bashir stood there with his mouth gaping, trying to figure a response for that, Dax said, "I'll get Sisko."

"If you would be so kind as to take his legs, Doctor," Garak said. He scooped up Eddington's considerable shoulders.

"If I didn't know you better," Bashir uttered, "I'd swear you were enjoying this, Garak."

"Not at all, Doctor. Though I admit, after three years of hemming dresses, a little action does seem a welcome change of pace."

Grunting with the effort of hauling Eddington into an anteroom, Bashir heaved, "I hope you'll still feel that an hour from now."

He straightened as Sisko and Dax came dashing into the main security area, which now looked quite innocent with Eddington snoozing merrily in the back, out of sight.

"Now," Sisko was saying even before he got to them, "first thing we have to do is get our hands on a runabout."

"It's already taken care of, Benjamin. Chief O'Brien is waiting for us at landing pad C with the *Rio Grande,* carrying a full complement of photon torpedoes."

"How did you know we'd be needing photon torpedoes?" Sisko asked her, with a tone that implied subterfuge and approval all at the same time.

Bashir watched them, always fascinated with this bizarre relationship between his commander and his fellow officer. Sisko wasn't saying anything, yet he wasn't exactly asking.

He was testing.

Bashir tensed with the importance of all this. If Sisko would force Dax to say aloud what she had deduced and acted upon, anticipating his personal logic, then there were strong actions in the offing.

The doctor didn't move. He looked from one to the other in the space of those two seconds.

Dax eyed Sisko too. "Because I know you. You want to make sure the Dominion stays on its side of the galaxy. The only way to do that is to blow up the entrance to the wormhole."

Bashir felt something in his chest snap. An astonishing act—a fabulous solution. The end of their careers, yet the one great action a person could take for what he believed in. What happened to a soldier who had sworn an oath, but whose leaders had made an immoral decision.

The doctor knew that indecent cooperation had been bought with a cloak of promotion for Commander Sisko, and he was here and now rejecting that. They all were.

The doctor searched Commander Sisko's face for the slightest doubt.

None.

"I'm glad we're all in agreement," Sisko said. His passive courage was heartening.

"Well," Bashir clipped, "I guess this means the end of our Starfleet careers."

"I wouldn't worry about that, Doctor," Garak said, as if he were one to talk.

Dax threw him a glance. "That's easy for you to say."

"You misunderstand me, Lieutenant," the Cardassian said. "All I meant was it's foolish to worry about your careers at a time like this. After all, there's a good chance we're about to be killed."

Bashir widened his eyes. "Is that supposed to make me feel better?"

The commander was checking the Promenade for Jem'Hadar guards. Apparently it was all clear, because he came back in and gestured to his miniature SWAT team.

"All right," he said, "let's get moving."

CHAPTER
17

"This seems to be some kind of locking mechanism."

Within the cradle of the caverns, Odo peered at the metal door that bewitched their tricorders and defied their chants.

Kira watched him with bottled impatience and choked down an urge to spit out the obvious. Of course it was a locking mechanism!

"I was thinking the same thing," she said instead. No point wrecking the last few minutes they had to work together.

"Interesting," Odo said. "The purpose of this door is not to keep people out, but rather to keep whatever's on the other side in."

Pausing in her impatience, Kira was suddenly filled with a whole new kind of curiosity—she hadn't thought of that. "I wonder what's behind there," she mumbled.

Ah, marvelous. Now she was the one uttering the painfully obvious.

"I suppose we'll find out," Odo muttered, preoccupied, "as soon as I can get this door open. . . ."

His hand dissolved into a silver spike, and he put the end into the lock. The spike went in a lot farther than it should have been able to.

Kira beat down a shiver. It was nauseating to watch Odo's hand go into the lock almost up to the elbow.

A mechanical lock—she heard the tumbler click.

Odo pulled his extremity back. On its way out, it turned back into a hand. "Step back, Major," he said.

She moved out of the way, allowing him to put his weight against the hefty metal barrier.

It creaked, but it did move. There weren't any blitzes of energy to pound Odo back. No forcefields.

Kira drew her weapon and looked in.

Three Jem'Hadar soldiers glared back at her, their weapons also out and up.

One of them nodded to her. "We've been expecting you, Major."

"Halt! Put down your weapons!"

The Jem'Hadar guards, two of them, materialized directly in front of Sisko, Dax, Bashir, and Garak as they charged toward landing pad C.

Sisko skidded to a stop. Dax almost piled into him. Bashir managed to shy to one side. Garak—

The Cardassian twisted toward the Jem'Hadar, but he had his eyes—and his phaser—on Sisko.

"By all means, Commander, do what he says."

Bashir, in his typical innocence, stared like a child. "Garak?"

"You heard me, Doctor."

I'll peel those scales right off him, Sisko thought as he lowered his phaser to the deck. He had to, or the others would take his hesitation as a cue to act against this traitor and those two ugly customers.

Horn-mad, he shifted his glare to Garak and let his silence speak.

Garak sauntered toward the Jem'Hadar, his phaser loose at his side.

"I'm glad to see everything's going according to plan."

The Jem'Hadar stooges blinked at him. "What plan is that?"

"Didn't anyone tell you? You see, I pretend to be their friend—then I shoot you."

His phaser came up. A plume of energy swallowed both Jem'Hadar.

Sisko plunged to retrieve his weapon, scooped up Dax's, and handed it to her. On the other side of the corridor, Bashir got his own.

"Well done, Garak," Sisko said.

"Just something I read once in a book."

Waxy and numb, Bashir sighed, "I'm sure."

"Look out!"

Dax shoved Bashir to one side and raised her weapon.

Sisko had to spin almost all the way around before he could see what she was talking about—

two more Jem'Hadar aiming down the corridor from around a corner. As the four conspirators returned fire, he pressed Bashir back and motioned Dax and Garak to fall back also. He aimed wild and hit one Jem'Hadar in the upper body.

Well, that was one. How many were there?

Sisko pressed Bashir back farther and fired again, not so wild this time, dodging return fire every step.

Clumsy because of his own heavy Cardassian build, Garak shoved Dax out of the way of a streak of energy, and couldn't clear it himself. One bolt glanced across his arm. The next—

Taking a blow full in the chest, Garak slammed into the bulkhead beside Dax and skidded to the deck.

"Garak!" Bashir howled.

He crossed Sisko's path toward the fallen Cardassian, right into the path of cross fire, toward Garak.

Under cover of fire from Sisko and Dax, he stooped at Garak's side.

"It looks like we won't be having lunch after all, Doctor," the Cardassian gurgled pitifully. He got all the words out. That was his last bit of luck before he died.

Sisko caught Bashir bodily and dragged him back. "It's too late, Doctor!"

As he pulled Bashir away, Dax provided more cover. Under the whine of constant weapons fire they shuffled toward the airlock.

"Come on!" Against his arm and side Sisko felt Bashir pull back toward Garak. The doctor didn't want to give up. What if Garak still had a shiver of life in him? What could it be like to leave him there like that?

Sisko knew. Knew and hated it.

The Jem'Hadar pressed them without relent toward the airlock, making the going slow. Constantly they had to duck close to the bulkheads as arrows of unshielded crackling energy pounded so close they could feel the buzz of cutting power against the fine hairs of their skin.

Dax got there first and hit the control panel. The airlock gate hummed open.

Sisko shoved Bashir inside, paused to fire one final blast out the open gate, then plunged inside. "Move it, Lieutenant!"

"Right behind you," Dax promised. She finished programming the panel so well that it wouldn't be able to be unprogrammed without a full emergency engineering squad. The gate buzzed shut between them and the Jem'Hadar with a grinding clang.

O'Brien was in the pilot's chair and Sisko dove for the cockpit. The runabout was already warmed up. Behind him he heard Dax and Bashir pile into their seats, lungs heaving.

"Get us out of here, Chief," he said.

The engineer cranked around to count heads. "What about Garak?"

"He's not coming," responded Bashir grimly.

O'Brien nodded in understanding. "Right. Hang on."

Sitting beside O'Brien as the runabout rose and wobbled in open space before sliding out of the station's perimeter at three times safe speed, Sisko pressed his shoulder blades against the back of his seat and forced himself to breathe evenly, to set an example for the others, to show that he believed, he *knew* they were doing the right thing. There was no *legal* obligation to protect a planet that hadn't yet taken all the steps into Federation membership, but that was a petty loophole. If the little girl next door was being torn apart by a pack of dogs, he didn't have a legal obligation to put his life on the line, go over there and kill the dogs. But anyone with an ounce of morality would hop the fence.

Funny how well the pack-of-dogs idea fit. The way the Jem'Hadar ships had come and surrounded the *Defiant* and chewed it to shreds . . .

In the side viewer, *Deep Space Nine* spooled against black space, chunky and inelegant, powerful and independent; its great arching docking pylons clawed both upward and down like the arms of some great beast.

He hadn't liked it when he'd first come here, but he'd taken the job for the sake of Jake. Now for the sake of Jake and a billion others he was leaving.

Jake would understand if he never came back. Garak was right—that chance was a good one, the best one.

If they lived, then he was definitely coming back. Life as a fugitive wasn't in the cards. His obligation was to come back and face court-martial and have his say about what was happening in the halls of the United Federation of Planets. It was wrong to cede any territory to the Dominion at this stage. Maybe at any stage. They were losing their sense of purpose, their linear concept of right and wrong, that which was elemental to basic freedom and the sovereignty of the individual.

He would come back and stand his trial and tell them all. And his son would see him do it, even if he did it in manacles.

And he would have shown Bajor that they were not alone, even if it was only the four of them in this runabout who were with them.

In a few minutes the Dominion will be sixty-seven years away. And the Federation will have time to think things out.

"Thirty seconds to wormhole," O'Brien said, and shook Sisko out of his thoughts.

"Prepare to launch photon torpedoes," Sisko ordered. The order came very easily. He didn't have to think twice—those moments were past.

"We're being hailed," Dax reported, keeping all emotion out of her voice. "It's Admiral Necheyev."

Sisko waited a beat, then reached forward and engaged his panel. He didn't say anything, but only waited until Necheyev appeared on the monitor next to him.

"Commander," Necheyev said with sharp reserve, "I'm ordering you to stand down. Return to the station immediately."

Well, now that *that* was over with, they could have a real conversation. The admiral was jaundiced with rage, which made her even more waxy and pale than normal. She was practically fading away.

"I'm afraid I'm going to have to refuse that order," Sisko said simply.

Borath lowered his nose. "Please, Commander. Don't make us send the Jem'Hadar after you."

Sisko almost laughed.

"Go right ahead," he granted. "But you'd better warn them not to expect any reinforcements for about seventy years."

He shut off the monitor. No point stretching the inevitable. They were already hopping mad at him.

He stretched back to enjoy it. That was all he had to enjoy.

The wormhole flashed awake before them, bright white-yellow-electric-blue with a punch right down the middle, an illusion of open space, like looking down the eye of a hurricane. Strange how it seemed to know when such a tiny ship came poking.

"The wormhole's opening," Dax said unnecessarily.

Sisko didn't acknowledge her. "Attack pattern theta, Mr. O'Brien. Then hard aport."

There was no pause. "Yes, sir."

In the shaved seconds during which bright photon salvos that looked like nothing more than balls of light flew out from the runabout and rifled toward the wormhole, Sisko saw visions of Odo and Kira and wondered if he was plastering shut their only escape from the Gamma Quadrant—yes, of course he was. That was exactly what he was doing. With these shots, he was betting his friends were dead. And if they weren't he was sacrificing them to life on the other side, in whatever manner they could cull out for themselves.

He wished he could explain to Kira. He wanted

her to know that her exile was for a reason, and that someone over here did care about Bajor and stand firm on the principles the Federation had always declared.

Simple statements. Not exactly Walt Whitman. But he wished he could say them to her anyway.

If he had any regrets, that was the one. Perhaps the gesture of closing the wormhole was enough. She would figure it out, wouldn't she?

The torpedoes tumbled freely into the core of the wormhole and, on their timed-release detonators, blew up.

A brilliant mushroom of destruction washed back across their viewscreens from the phenomenon that was barely beyond the theoretical. High glare came tumbling over them at a rolling boil. The *Rio Grande* surged backward like a toy on an ocean wave.

Sisko wanted to shout through the strain for everyone to hang on, but they were already doing that. He caught a glimpse of O'Brien's tensed arm and hand clawing on the pilot's seat. The explosion and residual shock waves piled out toward them and the longest puffs of it engulfed them, but the runabout remained intact and took the pounding.

Not so bad.

Sisko raised his head from the back of the seat. Still alive—

Another shock wave hit, harder this time. Had one of the salvos delayed its detonation?

No, that was closer!

"Chief—"

"It's the Jem'Hadar ship, Commander. It's left the station and it's headed our way."

"Hard about, Mr. O'Brien." He cranked around to let the others see the set of his eyes. "Battle stations, everyone. Strongest shields to 'em."

Before they completed their swing around, they took another hit.

"Shields down twenty percent," Dax calmly said.

Sisko didn't bother to acknowledge that. "Return fire!"

O'Brien did his best to dodge Jem'Hadar shots— at close range those bolts could disintegrate a ship this size.

"Dax, take over shield controls! Sacrifice the aft shield to fire power!" Sisko wheeled out of his chair and plunged back to handle weapons himself, while Dax stumbled toward the shield controls.

Damned peacetime design—everything in these runabouts was an arm's length and a quarter from everything else. It took four people to do four things.

No time off to be annoyed.

O'Brien was doing a fair job of making sure any bolt that hit them was a glancing blow; then he'd have to compensate for the hit and try to keep control over the skid.

"Try to target their thruster ports!" he shouted over the din of another glancing hit. The runabout whined around them as it swung on an invisible string and came up almost directly under the belly of the Jem'Hadar.

"Now, sir!" O'Brien called over the thunder of

another attack—this one was a near miss. *Rio Grande* only caught the backwash.

The Jem'Hadar ship couldn't aim directly underneath, apparently, at least not this design.

Sisko crammed his hands against the phaser mechanism and opened fire, scraping a line of blistering energy across the underside of the enemy ship.

"One thruster down, Benjamin," Dax said with a note of victory in her voice.

Small victory, but they would take it. The Jem'Hadar ship was crippled, but not down. And they weren't giving up, either.

Sisko could almost feel the fundamental revenge boiling at him from the enemy ship. They didn't have a reason to smash the runabout to bits, but that's what they were trying to do, just as they had destroyed the *Starship Odyssey* and the battleship *Defiant*. The only reason they hadn't done the same to the runabout was the tiny ship's size, speed, and ability to turn on a dime.

"How long can we keep this up?" he grumbled to himself. "Try to stay under them while I recharge!"

"Aye, sir." O'Brien had his back stiff, his teeth gritted, his eyes fixed on the enemy ship, and his hands full.

Ah, good old-fashioned sizzling provocation— Sisko sensed the gall of the Jem'Hadar and he liked it. If he had to die out here, he wanted to die making these animals feel the sting of a roused Starfleet. Even if they never went home, they'd never forget.

"I can't hold course!" O'Brien gasped.

Dax waved at the smoke between them. "Benjamin, we've lost our fuel pressure!"

Sweat sheeting his face, Sisko digested that and made a decision. "All right, everyone, this is it. We can't fight anymore. All we can do is take that ship down with us."

"Understood," Dax said. She wasn't surprised at all.

O'Brien had tears in his eyes. His voice didn't falter. "Aye-aye, sir."

Sisko turned to Bashir. "Doctor, do you understand too?"

Bashir gathered whatever he had left and all but took his own pulse. "Yes, sir," he said. "I understand."

"Good. I want you all to know the great honor it's been for me to serve with you. Chief O'Brien, come about, full speed. Collision course."

CHAPTER
18

KIRA GLARED down the barrel of the Jem'Hadar weapon and almost fired her own.

Pulling on all her experience in that first second, she held back. More than she wanted to kill the Jem'Hadar, she wanted to see what was in there. She had to be alive to do that.

And she was still alive. That meant they wanted her to see it too.

"Inside," one of the guards accommodated.

A dark, rocky tunnel . . . a score of Jem'Hadar soldiers flanking both sides. Fighting was out of the question. Odo could escape, but he evidently wanted to know the secret of this planet that had only minutes ago been his most hallowed place, spoiled by the presence of the Jem'Hadar and the lie his own people had apparently told him.

A hazy light shone at the far end of this tunnel.

Together, under the studious presence of Jem'Hadar guns, the two walked toward the light. They weren't going to be shot from behind. There was some other purpose to this parade.

Aware of Odo beside her, Kira wanted to stop him, turn and talk to him, tell him that she was with him no matter what, no matter how sour turned this party cake of life he had discovered, that he . . . that they would all . . .

Nope, nothing was good enough.

Something had gone haywire and she could see in the set of his mouth and sad browless eyes that he realized his paradise was withering.

His people had lied to him.

The two were ushered around a corner and bathed by the light, where they both stopped short.

"Please, come in."

Kira moved inside. The Jem'Hadar didn't even make any move to take her phaser away, but only herded her and Odo into an area with a high ceiling.

There she stopped so quickly she actually hurt her own ankle. And she stared like a fool.

The crew of the *Defiant* sat around a small interrogation room—Sisko, Dax, O'Brien, Bashir, T'Rul.

"Commander?" Kira blurted in relief and panic —were they dead? In suspension? "Dax!"

"They can't hear you," the Vorta man said.

Sisko and the others were hooked up in a circle, some kind of devices attached to their heads, monitored by Borath and two other Vorta from a bank of computer consoles. The Vorta was smiling passively. Kira almost kicked the smile in.

All the others were sitting attached to this hive of machinery, eyes closed, faces tense, jaws clenched. They were experiencing something.

Odo pushed forward. "What have you done to them?"

"Nothing harmful," Vorta said. "We're just conducting a little experiment."

Sounded damned casual. Kira approached her trapped crewmates. She could yank these mechanisms away from them, but what would that do to them? Was this some form of life support?

She looked at each of them to be sure each was alive—they were. Relief struck so hard that she almost fell down.

"What kind of experiment?" she asked.

"To see how they'd respond to an attempt by the Dominion to gain a foothold in the Alpha Quadrant." The Vorta wasn't as smug as usual. "We were curious to see how much they'd be willing to sacrifice in order to avoid a war with us."

Kira glanced at Odo, then back. "And . . . how are they doing?"

The Vorta sighed, then shrugged. "Unfortunately, they're proving to be as stubborn as I feared."

"I'm glad to hear it," Odo freely derided.

"Are you?" The Vorta's invidious arrogance popped back on like a light. "Well, that *is* a problem. But, thankfully, it's not one I have to solve."

"But I do."

Another voice entered the small drumming room, moving through the faint throb of electrical power and computer switching.

Kira stepped back just enough. Odo came forward.

The female shapeshifter strode toward them from an unseen entranceway.

Through unveiled shock Odo said, "I don't understand. You know about this?"

"Yes."

"But how could you allow it!"

The female puzzled over him, or was tormenting him with a pause—Kira couldn't tell which. They were certainly more complex beings than they wanted to let on. . . .

Almost on reflex, without thinking, Kira stepped forward herself and said, "She belongs to the Dominion. Don't you?"

The face so much like Odo's, for whatever reason, turned to her. "Belong to it? Major, the changelings *are* the Dominion."

Irreconcilable now, Odo gazed at her and carried logic a step further.

"You're the Founders," he said.

He seemed unaffected, but Kira knew he was doing that on purpose, so the shapeshifter and the others would see only his strength, and not his magnificent pain.

"Ironic, isn't it?" the female said. "We the hunted now control the destinies of hundreds of other races."

"But why 'control' anyone?" Odo demanded.

"Because what you can control can't hurt you. So

many years ago, we set ourselves the task of imposing order on a chaotic universe."

"Imposing order?" Kira blared. "Is that what you call it? I call it murder!"

"What you call it is no concern of ours."

Odo shook his head. "But how do you justify the destruction of the *Odyssey?* The deaths of all those people?"

"The solids have always been a threat to us. That's all the justification we need."

Furious in the face of raw, smug bigotry—she recognized it because she had done a little of that herself—Kira realized she was tensing to throw a punch or a slap or a spit when Odo came between her and the shapeshifter.

"These solids have never harmed you," he said, waving his long elegant hands toward Sisko, Dax, and the others held in this bizarre shooting gallery. "They travel the galaxy, looking to expand their knowledge, the same as you once did."

The female's body grew tense, her posture rigid. That, perhaps, was indignation.

"The solids are nothing like us," she said corrosively.

Depths of sadness came into Odo's expressionless face and rolled beneath its surface. He surveyed the being who had seemed to be exactly like himself, the symbol and presence of his great homecoming, his search of many lifetimes, and he saw for the first time the stunted substance below the form. Unlike their mythical physical evolution, these people's society had advanced to a certain point . . . and stopped dead.

Form to a shapeshifter was nothing, Kira realized as she watched the silent interplay. She watched and applauded in silence as Odo once and for all dropped the string he had held that had drawn him to these people.

"No, I suppose they're not," he said finally. "And neither am I. I've devoted my life to the pursuit of justice. But justice means nothing to you."

"It's not justice you desire, Odo," the female said. "It's order. The same as we do. And we can help you satisfy that desire in ways the solids never could." She raised her own hand and motioned to Sisko, still seated and involved in his fabricated dream. "This will all become clear to you once you've taken your place in the great link."

"No." He lifted his chin, an action decidedly solid. "I admit this link of yours is enticing. But you see, I've already formed a link . . . with these people." Without waiting for a response or seeming to care if he got one, Odo turned to the Vorta. "I want you to remove those devices from Commander Sisko and the others. Then bring them their comm badges."

The man stared at him, then looked for guidance to the female shapeshifter.

Kira watched with supreme pride as Odo stood before the shapeshifter, before all their people, and decided the truth. They had sent him out to bring knowledge and wisdom back, and to tell them what he saw and believed about the outside galaxy. When he had come back, they had belittled him for his experiences. If they chose not to accept the word of their own messenger, then who were the foolish?

The Vorta said, "We can't allow them to leave." He glanced at Kira. "They know too many of our secrets."

Kira licked her lips and prepared to explain that a big gooey lake and a planet where plants grew without a sun wasn't that much of a "secret" to keep—their "powers" weren't that impressive in a modern age. But Odo spoke again.

"I can't allow you to keep them here. They're leaving and so am I."

Again he gestured, this time much more compassionately, at his commander and crewmates, and there was nobility in his proclamation.

The shapeshifter searched his eyes. "It took you many years to find your way back home. Are you really willing to leave it again so soon?"

"Unless you intend to stop me."

His scrappy decree surprised her again.

"No changeling has ever harmed another," she said.

"Until now," Odo bluntly told her. "Because whatever you do to them you're going to have to do to me."

Kira held her breath.

Odo and the shapeshifter examined each other, conviction for conviction, for what seemed a long time, long enough that Kira had to hold her arms straight at her sides to avoid lashing out, ripping those attachments off her commander and the people she had minutes ago thought were dead. She had expected to have to go back and report the slaughter of these friends of hers, to report the failure of the *Defiant*.

Where was the ship? Destroyed?

She clamped her mouth shut and didn't ask, didn't interfere.

The female shapeshifter watched Odo for a long time. He wasn't backing down. He didn't intend to stay "home"—because it wasn't his home. He was rejecting instinct. To be bound by form was to be primitive and tribal. What bound people was their common principle.

Kira felt a twinge of guilt. How often had she been Bajoran first and principled later?

Then, as simply as the shapeshifters did everything else, the female turned to the Vorta man and said, "They're free to go."

Kira drew a breath to cheer her victory.

But the Vorta was staring at the shapeshifter, not doing as she had been told.

The shapeshifter turned cold and said, "Do you question my decision?"

After a dangerous few seconds, the man backed down. "The Vorta serve the Founders in all things."

He and the two other Vorta began removing those devices from their prisoners. They did so with studious deliberation, no longer looking up or questioning even in the slightest manner.

"Thank you," Odo said to the shapeshifter.

"Next time," she told him, "I promise you we will not be so generous."

"Constable?"

Kira and Odo turned at the same time. Moving

in his chair, Commander Sisko was blinking and forcing himself to come out of the haze imposed by these machines. Beside him, O'Brien was looking around too, and Dax and T'Rul—the hypnosis was falling away.

What had they been forced to experience? Kira moved forward so they could see her too and get the idea that they shouldn't try to fight, that the situation was still complicated.

"What happened to the *Rio Grande?*" O'Brien asked.

"The last thing I remember is collapsing the wormhole," Dax said, by way of an answer.

Kira gaped at her. Collapsing the wormhole! Then they were trapped here—

"The last thing I remember was being shot by some Jem'Hadar soldier," T'Rul muttered, glaring suspiciously at the two of those kind who stood in the background. Luckily she had the sense to restrain herself.

Sitting in a dim rocky room, in a gaggle of mechanical equipment, with a half-dozen life-forms standing around, was enough to give anyone pause.

Kira remained tense. Sisko wasn't ready to take over authority yet. He was trying to stand up, still foggy, fighting to understand what was happening as the Vorta went to each of them and handed them their comm badges.

"I'm sure it all seemed very real," she said carefully, waiting to be contradicted, "but the truth is you've been held in this room ever since the Jem'Hadar brought you here from the *Defiant.*"

Nobody told her she was wrong.

"Eris?" Blinking at the Vorta, Sisko supported himself first on the arm of his chair and then on Kira as she reached out to him. "What the hell is going on here?"

"Your ship is in orbit," Eris said. "You may transport to it whenever you're ready."

Kira could see that the answer wasn't enough for him. It wasn't really an answer. It was a twisted suggestion with a gauze of warning over it.

She watched Sisko. Was he awake enough to pick that up?

"Return to the *Defiant*, Commander," Odo chanced. "I'll be along shortly."

"Do as he says, sir," Kira abridged, hoping Sisko wouldn't notice that they were giving him orders without explanations. Most commanders didn't stand for that—not for long, anyway. "I'll stay down here with him and see that he gets back to the ship."

Sisko looked at her, then at Odo again, then scoped the motley gaggle around them.

He started to speak, but Bashir beat him to it.

"It's another shapeshifter!" the doctor burst, staring at the female.

Sisko looked at the female, clearly seeing that things were drastically changed, and he was obviously holding back questions and orders, waiting to understand.

"Commander," Odo said firmly, "you must leave now. I promise you I'll explain everything later."

With a gush of relief Kira noted Sisko motioning Dax, O'Brien, and T'Rul into a transporter pattern. The ship's automatic setting would do what he said now, using his comm badge as a fix. She stepped away, out of the pattern.

"I'll look forward to it, Constable," Sisko said, connecting significantly with Kira also before he straightened his shoulders and touched his comm badge. "Sisko to *Defiant*. Five to beam up."

"Commander, what on God's green growing earth was all that!"

O'Brien spun off his transporter pad and almost fell off the platform trying to get around in front.

Ben Sisko held his hands out to his crew to stay calm and take a deep breath.

"Dax, damage report," he ordered. "O'Brien, status of the wormhole."

"Checking, sir!" O'Brien ran for the sensor access panel.

Bashir was charmingly befuddled. "Was it all a dream? We didn't really blow up the wormhole?"

"All right, everyone calm down." Sisko looked around at the intact bulkheads of the tough little *Starship Defiant.* "Ship's still here . . . I thought Borath was lying. Apparently we never made it back to Alpha Quadrant at all. That means we didn't blow up the wormhole."

"Oh, come on!" O'Brien wailed. "We were there! I launched the photons myself. . . ." His panel whistled at him and he looked down, then shook his head and silently damned what he saw for some kind of trick. "Wormhole is intact, sir—twirling just as happy as anything. It's just as if we never . . ." His effort petered away as he began to doubt his own memory.

"Damage report," Dax said, "shows the same level of damage just before we abandoned ship, but there have been some automatic system repairs and some work done on the ship to make it spaceworthy. We're holding stable orbit. Warp engines have been jury-rigged." She looked up. "Eris and her people, possibly?"

"Or our people," Sisko guessed. "Kira and Odo weren't hooked up to all that machinery down there, were they? Did anyone see something I didn't?"

"I don't think they were," Dax agreed. "Eris didn't have to hand them their comm badges—"

"And they weren't disoriented, sir," Bashir added. "At least not at the same time we were."

Sisko nodded. "And they seemed to know what was going on down there."

He could see that Dax was more excited than she was letting on to the others as she said, "That means they escaped from *Defiant* before we were captured, and something different happened to them than what happened to us."

"What is this about blowing up the wormhole?" T'Rul demanded. She rounded on Sisko. "You would never dare such a thing!"

Sisko ignored her and turned to O'Brien and pointed at him. "The runabout *Rio Grande,* correct?"

O'Brien peered at him, nervous. "Yes, sir . . ."

"Federation pulling out of Bajor?"

"Yes . . ."

"Admiral Necheyev—and I was under arrest?"

"Oh, yes, sir. . . ."

He swung around to Dax. "Handing guardianship of Bajor over to the Founders?"

Dax nodded slowly. "The Founders, who were supposedly Eris and the other Vorta."

"Yes!" Sisko said. "How do you suppose we all had the very same dream?"

"It never happened?" Bashir swelled. He clapped a hand to his chest, sank back, and started silently ticking off all the other things that probably didn't happen. He peered at O'Brien, scouring for signs of a beating.

The engineer frowned at him and leaned away, but didn't say anything.

"So it was all a dream," Dax concluded. "All for nothing."

"It must be the next step above holodeck technology," O'Brien said. "Except you don't have to create form or sensation. You just feed the experience directly into the brain."

"It never happened?" Bashir followed. "But why? What's the good of that?"

T'Rul spun in place, anger limning her harsh features. "There is no 'good,' engineer. We were duped. Pawns!"

O'Brien squinted at her. "Oh, shut up, woman."

She raised her arm to backhand him, but Sisko caught it in midair and shoved her away.

"As you were," he snapped. "Just a minute. Let me think about this. . . ."

Touching the transporter mechanism, the bulk-heads, the consoles to assure himself the ship was indeed here with him, Sisko moved away from them, forcing his groggy mind to think.

"Not a dream," he said. "A test. And not for nothing. The moment you leave a dream, it becomes a shadow of reality. But I remember all of this. All our senses were there. They fed us the situation, and we reacted. We even interacted and said things to each other, didn't we?"

He spun around, and each of his people confirmed with a nod, and Bashir punctuated, "Oh, yes."

"We had the *same* dream. And those were all life-forms from the Gamma Quadrant," Sisko went on. "I'm assuming the shapeshifter is from here too—we'll get that out of Odo."

"You bet we will," O'Brien tossed in.

"How many other shapeshifters do you think there were?" Bashir asked.

"It was Odo's situation," Sisko said. "You saw Kira's expression. They knew what was going on and they didn't want us to bust the tightrope they were walking."

Dax came toward them from the console that still chirped for attention. "Think about the situation we were forced to experience. Why would—"

Bashir snapped his fingers. "They were trying to find out what we would do if the Federation could be convinced to abandon the wormhole!"

He held his breath suddenly and stared back and forth from Sisko to O'Brien, wondering if they'd done the right thing.

"And abandon Bajor, too," O'Brien put in. "Don't forget that."

"I'm not forgetting, Chief," Sisko said. "They were using us."

Adding up the fragments and mortaring the gaps, he prowled the deck, shaping the air before him with his hands as he paced.

"We were linked together, doing what we really would've done if those things had happened. It was one hundred percent as if we'd experienced it—the feelings, the smells—it was no dream. They wanted us to back down when faced with the prospect of abandoning this sector. To do it and just wilt away." He turned and pointed at each of them just as he had a few moments earlier, but with a new meaning this time. "But we didn't. We turned our backs on everything we know and the oaths we swore in order to do what was right. We proved that at least *some* factions in the Federation would refuse to buckle—possibly the whole Federation. After all, they were feeding us whatever Necheyev and Starfleet Command were doing. I say it *did* happen, in all but physical form." He balled a fist and pounded the transporter column. "And I'll bet they understand that."

He paused, and thought about his original mission into this quadrant—how he'd wanted to search for the Founders and instead had found his own purpose of soul. He'd been willing to give his life for this purpose, so billions of others could live in safety, and so his son could say, "Yes, my father did that."

Until now, Ben Sisko hadn't been sure he had that in him.

He swung around easily and felt his face crack into a devilish grin.

"They don't even realize it," he said, "but the Dominion has done us a favor. They didn't get what they wanted, but we got a chance to fight, *and* a second chance. We may well have bought time for the Federation by showing these people that we're not going to shy away."

"Then . . . you'd do it again," Bashir prodded. Not exactly a question. Not *exactly*.

At that Sisko stopped his pacing. He turned to the doctor and the others of his crew, and to the Romulan who had come to work a machine and ended up witnessing a revolution.

"You bet I would," he said.

CHAPTER
19

STILL ACHING FROM HER WOUNDS, favoring one arm and breathing in shallow puffs, Kira stayed at a respectful distance from the silver lake's edge.

At the grassy edge, Odo stood with the female shapeshifter.

When they'd first come to this planet, Kira remembered noticing how much like Odo these shapeshifters appeared.

Now they looked nothing like him to her. Nothing at all.

"I hope one day you'll return to us, Odo," the female was saying, "and take your rightful place within the Dominion."

Odo wasn't looking at the lake. He wasn't moved by it anymore. "I don't think that's possible."

The female surveyed him thoughtfully. "Your

link to the solids won't last. You'll always be an outsider."

"Being an outsider isn't so bad," he said. "It gives me a unique perspective. It's a pity you've forgotten that."

"Then perhaps one day I'll come and visit you. The Alpha Quadrant seems racked with chaos. It could use some order."

"Imposing your brand of order on the Alpha Quadrant may be more difficult than you imagine," Odo said, and there was a clear bolt of pride in his voice.

Kira saw the pride, and she warmed to it. These people weren't Odo's people. He had figured that out, and now she knew it too. Dax had talked about blowing up the wormhole. That machine had been some kind of simulator, drawing Commander Sisko and the others into a scenario that demanded the ultimate actions upon their creeds. She didn't have the details yet, but these weren't the kind of people to just *talk* about blowing up the wormhole if they thought it was the right thing to do.

They had acted it out. They thought they had done it. And there was only one reason for them to do something like that.

The commander had come through on more than his oath to Starfleet and the Federation. He had acted on his promise to her and the struggling people of Bajor that they wouldn't be shunted to the back burner of Benjamin Sisko's command.

Kira wanted to hear the details, but in a way she didn't need to. Yet she knew it wasn't true that all the answers a person was searching for weren't always in your own backyard. Sometimes they were seventy thousand light-years away.

"We're willing to wait until the time is right," the female was saying to Odo.

Odo gazed at her, unwavering. "And when will that be?"

But the female only smiled her beguiling smile. "I will miss you, Odo. But you will miss us even more."

Without giving him a chance to respond, she swirled into a starlight-jeweled pillar, elongated, and plunged back into the lake with the others of her kind.

On the lakeshore, Odo stood gazing out over the puddle of his ancestry.

Kira couldn't read the set of his shoulders as she came up behind him. Was he having doubts?

"Odo?" she began slowly, without really knowing what else she could say.

But he turned to her, and there was no doubt, no regret in his face. He hadn't taken the bait, the tease. His search was over.

"I'm ready, Major."

Kira looked for hesitation in his eyes, but there was none. She reached out and took his hand, burying the surprise in his face with a touching squeeze.

She touched her comm badge.

"Kira to *Defiant*. Two to beam up."

Sisko held back a grin of relief when he heard that. Two to beam up, not one. Odo was coming with them.

The light of satisfaction nearly blinded him. He had come into this quadrant to head off a war by showing his willingness to fight if he had to. And that's exactly what had happened. And he'd made contact. That was something too.

Two columns of energy appeared on the bridge—good. Dax was beaming them directly to their stations. That way, the ship could veer out of orbit immediately. He knew they'd better scat before something turned sour again or the "Founders" changed their little liquid minds.

That same relief washed over everyone as the columns materialized into Kira and Odo. Sisko saw in his crewmates' faces the overwhelming shock and pure luck that they were all together again.

But there was more. They were a fraction more settled with each other than before. They knew the sacrifice they had been willing to make—and in fact *had* made.

T'Rul made an effort to look smug as Kira smiled and took her station and Odo came to join Sisko on the command deck. Yes, the Romulans too would get a message that wouldn't break out any celebration bottles. They ran on the supposition that the Federation would weaken in time.

This wasn't the time. The Federation had proven up to the task, and the cloak had been proven secondary to what happened. T'Rul was having a bad day.

"Take us home, Lieutenant," Sisko said to Dax, and maybe he pressed an inflection on the word *home*.

"Yes, sir," she said, answering the inflection as much as the order.

Sisko looked to his side, to Odo, who stood gazing at the rogue planet, the dark dot on the night sky of a foreign quadrant.

"Constable," Sisko began slowly, "we have a lot to talk about."

Odo continued looking at that planet, and even after the ship turned away and warped back toward the wormhole, toward home, he continued to gaze in that same manner—not as though he'd lost something, but as though he'd found it.

"You're right, Commander," he sanctioned. "We do."

EPILOGUE

"APPROACHING THE WORMHOLE, Commander. It's almost over."

Dax's milky announcement lathered the bridge with hope, meant as it was for all of them and not just Sisko.

Calm, cautious victory undergirded the *Defiant*'s bridge. They had gone on a wild mission into the darkness, carrying only that one tiny match, and they were returning to tell of it.

Not a story of resounding success, but of rudimentary contact and of a chance to go forward. A *chance*.

That was all any pioneer hoped for as any frontier opened.

Dax had been right. Facts of frontiers had always read like this. Not of giant, heroic leaps, but of a thousand small and probing steps by the multitude of the daring.

"Sir?"

Sisko blinked out of his affair with the forward screen.

Beside him, Kira stood with one foot casually up on the command-chair pedestal.

"Major? A problem?"

"Oh, no, sir, no problem at all."

"Good. I didn't want a problem."

"No, sir, no," she said. "Everything's absolutely fine."

"Good."

He tried to let her off the hook, to sit in the command chair in companionable musing, but Kira wanted to say something and she wouldn't go away.

After a few moments of polite torture, Sisko said, "Say it, Major."

Smiles broke out and Kira rolled her eyes at him.

"Sir," she attempted again, "I just want to say . . . I'd like to say thank you."

"Oh?" He kept his voice low. "You're welcome, but why was that so difficult?"

She pushed herself to arm's length and looked at the floor long enough to gather herself.

"It's not so difficult to say. It's difficult to get it all into two words." Now she looked up at him. The smile had gone, and there was a deep credence in her bright, troubled eyes. "I think Bajor is going to feel a little less alone in the galaxy after this, thanks to you."

Sisko offered her a humble nod. "For a while I thought we'd lost Bajor to the Jem'Hadar. I didn't like it, Major. From now on I'm going to step on more toes, pull more strings, and ring more bells to get resources dedicated to this corner of space. If the Federation thinks I've complained too much up until now, they're going to wish the Jem'Hadar had kept me."

Despite the undertones, he managed to get a flash of cheer out of her, and out of himself. They were both heartened by the prospect of stepping on bureaucratic toes now that they had the leverage of their brashness to do so. They had put their own lives on the line, they had done that which no one said could, should, be done, and nobody had any I-told-you-so's to hold over their heads.

Kira eyed him cannily. "Won't be long before you're as stubborn and bickering as the rest of us Bajorans, will it?"

Wondering if she'd be offended if he laughed, Sisko held his elbows against his ribs and paused.

But she was scoping him in that Peter Pan way she had, and she was smiling.

"We work pretty hard on that image," she said.

So they laughed together.

"I'll practice, Major."

Pocket Books
Hardcover presents a
deluxe collectors' edition

STAR TREK®
"WHERE NO ONE HAS GONE BEFORE"™
A History in Pictures

Text by J. M. Dillard
*With an introduction by
William Shatner*

**Available at
to a bookstore
near you**

POCKET
BOOKS

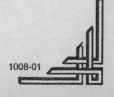

1008-01